Collection of Short Stories 2023

Porscha A. Aubrey

Collection of Short Stories 2023

Creative Writing Club

Published by Porscha Aubrey

Ottawa, ON K1N 8K2

Creative Writing Club is a small publishing company based in Ottawa, Ontario

ISBN (Paperback): 978-1-7390436-2-9

ISBN (Hardcover): 978-1-7390436-1-2

ISBN (eBook): 978-1-7390436-0-5

First Edition: February 2024

Printed in Canada

I dedicate this collection of short stories to my friend/old classmate Dorian Bansoodeb that lives at .... You asked me to put you as a cool character in a story, well then how about an entire collection? Oh, and a short story.

Thank you for making class tolerable and amazing, you are smart, talented, and kind and there were even times that a simple joke you'd make had made my entire day.

I wish you luck with your studies and am rooting for you! Keep up the hard work and continue trying to stay positive in this economy!

Warning

This novel features contents that may be seen as harmful or triggering. Reader's discretion is advised.

Table Of Contents

The Reality Of Fantasy   1

Burnt Bean Juice   5

Deathchill: Short Story   12

Pyro Hero   16

Care For The Baby   24

Indecent Breaths Of Nature   26

Sky Guardians   27

The Guidance Of Numuin   32

Particle   43

Down With Them Youngins   47

Scarlet, Azure   58

Give Everything, End Up With Nothing   61

Goodbye, My Loved Ones   65

Complete Fantastical Logic   71

Just In Case   75

Comfort Cabin   78

Whispers Of Shadows And Light   80

Cyn-mas   84

Veiled Blade   86

Disciple Two : A Shrouded Personas Short Story   89

The Reality of Fantasy

"Alex, you have to listen to me very closely," A feminine voice speaks with a hurried tone.

My eyes drift open and I find myself in space, well, a grassy platform in space. The stars glint and shine around me, like trillions of eyes gazing upon my soul. The grass is dusty and brittle, much like it's a land stuck in a dry spell. My back is sore and head pounding, with a grunt, I sit up and search for a figure to attach the voice to. But all there is is emptiness.

"There has been an error," The voice continues. "You have gained a sixth sense due to a mistake in time and space."

"That's my fault," A doopy sounding male voice adds. "Sorry."

"Yeah, this idiot decided to mess around with astrology people and ended up knocking the lineup of stars all out of place," The feminine voice sternly mentions. "But we must warn you before you awaken. When you wake up, you will have the ability to see into another realm. You must be careful though, because your body will be in two places at once and you will need to learn how to manoeuvre through both worlds."

I attempt to speak, to ask questions, but not a single word comes out. Instead, I struggle to breathe, my body numb. When will I return to normal? I contemplate my question, hoping they are able to read my mind in some sort of way.

"We don't know."

My body shoots up, lungs gasping for air and eyes darting around searching for differences. Except, everything is the same. My bookshelf is still full of dust and unread novels, my clothes are still all over my floor, all of my cups and plates are still on my desk and bedside table. Nothing is different. I look at my arms and legs, there are cuts on them from when I was messing around with my friends a few days ago, but they're still their usual fair skin tone. No claws either, and I'm not setting myself on fire, which is good since this blanket was really expensive.

My legs are as stiff as boards, making me walk like a lego man towards my door. Stopping in front, with a Marvel poster staring back at me, I place my hand on the doorknob and immediately remove it, wincing. It's freezing and burning at the same time. Using my shirt as a cover, I grip the knob again and yank the door open, jaw-dropping upon seeing what's on the other side. There is a tiny human wearing bright red scales riding a black dragon, people are striking each other with lighting, healing each other with various colours of light.

I slam the door, shutting my eyes and breathing heavily. This can't be real. I must be asleep. There's no way this is reality. Pinching and slapping myself, leaving red marks all over my body, I realise that this is reality, and I'm screwed.

Opening the door again, I step outside, gazing upon the vast world. Gotta keep this door open, based on the movies I've seen, if that door shuts then I'm trapped here forever. Taking a step forward, I walk face first into a forcefield of some sort.

"Right, I'm in two worlds," I mumble, rubbing my nose and placing my hands on what is supposed to be the walls of my hallway. My fingers run along the invisible stone as I guide my feet along a pathway towards a town in the distance. In a few more steps I should be in my living room. Wait, can people in my world still see me? Guess I'll find out eventually.

With each step I become more comfortable with guiding myself, after all, I've been walking this route everyday. Though very soon I'm going to have to leave my place and start going down some stairs, but it looks like a downhill is coming up too, so I should be fine.

The hair on my skin rises, turning hard and sharp like knives. Is my body already turning and adjusting to this world? If so, can the people in my world see what's going on with me? So many questions, and by the looks of it, those voices are unable to answer any of them.

Everything is both cold and hot at the same time, which makes sense, it's late fall in my world, and by the looks of it, summer in this one. The dragon in the sky lands in the centre of the town off in the distance and both sides stop their fight and their far away bodies turn and stare at me.

"I'm so dead," I mumble, watching as some of them start to sprout wings and take flight.

I attempt to run away, but promptly trip over what I assume is my sofa. Before my body registers it, red hands and claws are wrapping around my limbs and lifting me up. I attempt to grip onto my sofa, but the moment their skin touches mine, the furniture disappears entirely. Ducking my head, preparing for impact, shock goes through me as I realise that there are no longer walls or a ceiling. What happened to my world? Am I trapped here now? Gazing back, I realise that the door to my room is gone now too.

I scream and attempt to kick the red scaly people but they're unfazed. Their touch doesn't hurt me in any way, shape, or form. In fact, it feels more like they're using their claws to help keep me in secured than to dig into me.

They begin to glide, descending into the town where the dragon sits perched atop a roof. Upon touching the ground, I drop to my knees, arms wrapped around my head, screaming at the top of my lungs. I can feel them circling around me, feel my body tense up and hair goes sharp, feel their eyes on me from all angles.

"The pale being has returned!" The red armoured, dragon-riding person cheers.

Slowly, I remove my hands from my head and sit up, gazing around me at the large crowd that has formed. Some of them cover their faces with masks, others have horns all over their body's. But even then, I can tell that every single one of them is consumed with joy.

The crowd erupts into cheers, some of them send balls of fire into the sky, forcing them to explode much like fireworks. Two people with ice form a large statue that looks exactly like me. People start setting up tables of food and drinks, designed like a buffet in a forest.

"What- what's going on?" I mumble, taking the hand of the armoured person.

"Grab a plate first, then I will explain everything," They guide me to the table, handing me a warm wooden plate.

"Who are you?" I ask, cautiously filling up my plate. Surely all of this must be poisoned.

"I am named Tyfu Ghun," He states proudly, grabbing a huge leg of meat from some sort of unknown animal and slamming it onto his plate. "I am the chosen guardian of this realm, given all of the powers in the universe in order to protect and lead my people."

"So, you're like, the main character?" I ask, taking a few chicken wings and a salad.

Tyfu and a few other people erupt into laughter around me, "Ah yes, we've heard of those fantasy novels shared in other realms, we have a few here as well."

"Yeah, history books," One of the citizens grumbles, two bodies behind me.

We reach the end of the buffet line and I'm handed a glass of water with a strange-looking fruit in it. Like a dragon fruit but a yellowy-green and a shit ton of spikes that I see the others snacking on.

"It's for good-luck," Tyfu says, noticing me staring at the people snacking. "It's somewhat a spiritual belief of ours, the nature gives us power. Us caring for it and feeding from it is what gives us our powers."

Tyfu leads me to a quieter area of the celebration so then we can actually hear one another, he lifts his open hand in the air and two seats shoot up from the ground. I take one, setting my plate and drink on the large armrests, focusing on the person sitting next to me.

"So what is going on?" I get straight to the point, stunning Tyfu with my tone of voice.

He takes a large bite out of the meaty leg and sets down his plate. Each second of chewing is another increase of my heart rate. "You must listen very closely. We've been waiting for this day for years, ever since you were taken from us."

"Huh? What do you mean?" I furrow my brows, cracking my knuckles.

"That world you've spent so much of your life in, you're not from it," Tyfu calmly explains.

"Well yeah, I'm from Canada and started living in America when I turned five," I gulp, hoping that that was all he was trying to explain.

"You must not continue with that closed mind," Tyfu shakes their head. "If you continue to make excuses then you will have a far more difficult time understanding the truth."

"Just tell me then," I mumble, eyes focused on the detail of the wooden seats below us.

"You are from here, but you were taken away by the stars," The armoured person wearing red dragon scales tells me.

"Huh? Why?" I blink, not sure what to think.

"Because you looked different than the rest of us," Tyfu gestures towards the crowd not too far from us, they all stop and smile for a moment before going back to their food and chatter.

"So let me get this straight," I hold my hands up in front of me, trying to process the information however much I can. "I was born here, in this strange realm." Tyfu nods and I gesture to myself. "But because I look like this, I was taken away by the stars that I'm pretty sure I had a conversation with just an hour ago, and I lived out my life with a bunch of random people that look similar to me?"

Tyfu nods again, then adds, "Look at your arms, do you really think a normal 'human being' could have their hair be as sharp as knives?"

"Huh," I breathe, discreetly pinching myself once more, but still nothing happens. "I always figured that it was just because I was in this world." Tyfu shakes his head and I take a sip of my drink. "Hm, I should've read more books growing up."

Burnt Bean Juice

Christmas music is playing throughout the shop, 'Baby It's Cold Outside' is giving the feeling of lonely solitude to the only people in the shop. The male barista sits by a TV playing the video of a fireplace and sipping a hot chocolate overflowing with whipped cream. His stubble beard carrying a small dollop of whipped cream, his long, brown hair tied up in a ponytail, and hazel eyes drawing me in with every glance. I look away, my cheeks burning red, my extra thick hot chocolate is keeping my hands warm while my heart is freezing on this lonesome Christmas day. Other people are spending time with their families, couples are going on romantic walks and children are having snowball fights with their friends. Meanwhile, I'm here, alone. How did I end up here? I used to be busy every year, but because of the pandemic, I can't spend time with anyone I love.

The scent of a freshly brewed pot of coffee sends me into a trance. I stare out the window, watching the snow coming down, the teenagers are pushing each other into the huge banks that children usually slide down. A family walks by, two women, a dog, and a little boy. The women are walking hand-in-hand, smiling lovingly at each other, and the boy hugs his dog. A little bit of snow falls onto the dog's snout, causing it to sneeze, the child squeals from laughter, his smile adding a little bit of joy to my emptiness.

My eyes adjust and I'm now looking into my reflection, my half-up half-down golden blond hair is frozen at the tips, my cheeks bright and rosy, my skin is pale from the lack of sun. Other than my sad gaze, you'd think I was ready for a photo shoot.

A timer dings and the barista heads over to the oven, putting on some gloves, he opens it up and pulls out a batch of freshly baked chocolate chip cookies. The scent is absolutely phenomenal, it reminds me of when I was six and my mother and I spent all day baking while my father set up a snow fort outside for me. My favourite gift that Christmas would definitely be the laughter and joy, or the puppy, I loved that puppy.

"Want some?" A voice asks over my shoulder. I jump, sent out of my trance. The barista smiles at me kindly, his voice is deep and manly like he's about to order an army of troops.

I stutter, "Y-yes, thank you." I take a warm cookie off of the plate and bite down into it. A hot chunk of chocolate pours into my mouth, causing me to salivate. It's even more delicious than I thought.

The man places the plate down and then places his hand on the seat next to me, asking with his kind yet deep voice, "May I join you?"

I struggle to speak for a moment but manage an, "Of course." I gesture to the seat and he joins me. "Why are you working on Christmas day?"

"Long story," He grunts as he sits down and chomps down onto a cookie, a chunk of cookie falls onto his lap and he wipes it off.

"Well, it's not like I'm busy," I joke taking a sip of my hot chocolate.

"Well, my little brother thought it would be an amazing idea to bring his pet rat into the shop and let him try some of his food," the barista started. I try to act amazed and serious but I accidentally blurt out a giggle. He chuckles, "Yeah, I laughed first as well. So a Karen ended up coming in at the time, and she saw the rat."

I perk up and twist my entire body towards him, showing complete interest, "This should be good."

He smiles, "She saw the rat and started smacking it with her purse, and when the rat fell off the counter and started running around the shop she was screaming, 'It bit me! It bit me!'"

I roll my eyes, "And what happened next."

"Surprisingly my boss took my brother's side and told the Karen to get out because of how she was treating a living creature," the man nodded in amusement. "But since I didn't tell my brother to leave or not let his rat run around, so I was forced to work overtime for the entire time that my boss tries to fix the cafe's reputation."

"Is the rat alright?" I ask him, concerned.

"Oh yeah, the rat is better than ever, it landed on the floor like a cat," the man reassured me. "Oh, by the way, my name's Matt, what's yours?"

"Sahri," I respond.

"That's such a beautiful name, does it mean anything?" He asks me, dipping a bit of his cookie into his hot chocolate.

"It's Arabic," I answer. I let out a bright laugh when a chunk of his cookie falls into his hot chocolate. "It means magical." We both laugh, "I know, I know, it's silly."

Matt beams, "No, it's beautiful" We both blush and avoid eye contact for a minute. I, only then, started paying attention to every detail of the cafe. A large blackboard is on the wall just above the coffee machines, it's tinted from the several different colours of chalk, it's certainly due for a wash. A painting of a majestic forest is nailed onto the brick wall, it looks brand new, it must've been freshly dusted. The coffee machine sends off the mixed feeling of pulling an all-nighter to work on a project and relaxing by a fireplace and reading a novel. We gaze back towards each other, our eyes twinkling from the light of the fake fireplace, "What are you doing here on Christmas day? You were here all day."

"Pandemic," I respond nonchalantly. "Literally everyone in my family is vulnerable except for me, so I'm all alone."

"What about friends?" Matt asks me curiously, furrowing his brow. His handsome face, looking serious, intimidating, yet also caring and concerned.

"They're all either busy, in a different country, or spending time with family and their boyfriend or girlfriend," I exclaim, trying to not look as lonely as I am.

"What kind of stuff do you usually do on Christmas?" He asks me, sliding the plate over to me, it only has one cookie left. I break it in half and eat mine, sliding the other half over to him.

"My parents would wake up at five and start blasting my favourite Christmas songs. Then at six, they would come up to my room and start singing and dancing right next to my bed until I wake up. Once I finally wake up, my dad would get a snowball and throw it at me, after that he would run out of my room and I'd chase after him. He would run into his room then turn around and throw me onto his bed and start tickling me. After a few minutes, he would throw me over his shoulder and carry me downstairs where the entire house looks like something out of a dream. Seriously, it would look like the North Pole. There would be an army of nutcrackers, sweets set out on the coffee table, elves in every corner of the house, and the entire house would be covered in tinsel and other tree decorations. Then, my mother would put on a Christmas movie and we would all sit down and open Christmas gifts," I explain, feeling like I was reliving the moments as I was talking. "What about you?"

"Mine certainly is not as magical as yours," Matt laughs, squinting with his smile.

"I'm sure it will still be interesting," I hype him up.

"Well, my parents usually sleep until two in the afternoon, so my siblings and I would open our gifts together," he starts. I continue to gaze into his eyes, showing him every bit of interest I can. "So we would all wake up at like five and run downstairs, I would hand out the gifts while everyone else sips their hot chocolate and play fight. I always love seeing their faces light up after they open their gifts, they may be my siblings but I feel like a proud parent every time."

"How many siblings do you have?" I ask, expecting the range to be between three and twenty.

"Seven," he responds, chuckling at my astonished face.

"That must be a lot of gifts!" I shout, grinning from ear-to-ear.

"Actually my family doesn't make that much money, so it's only one gift per person, and I stopped getting gifts when I was fourteen," Matt responds, trying to not make it sound sad. "Decorations are a minimum as well, only the little lights and whatever everyone has made at school."

"I guess that does help keep you humble," I nod, trying to stay focused on the positives. "What do you guys do after your parents wake up?"

"I would make everyone an early dinner, and we would all make our parents a homemade gift," Matt notices my confusion and explains. "For instance, one year we made them a giant picture frame. So we all decided on a shape, which was a star. I would get the wood, shape it and everything, then the younger kids would paint and decorate it and everyone else would plan out an elaborate location and costumes and that for us to take the picture at."

"That is just adorable," I blush.

His face begins to turn red, and his smile looks genuinely happy and he laughs, "Our lives are so different."

"I bet your siblings love you deeply," I gaze into his eyes and smile lovingly.

"You should've seen my parent's reaction when my little sister used me as her role model for a school project," he grins from thinking about it. "They sat me down and asked me how I'm so amazing and then thanked me for being there for them."

"Did they feel bad?" I smiled at him with a hint of remorse in my eyes. His are glistening, he might be holding back tears but even so, the shining causes him to look even more beautiful with every passing second.

"No, they were grateful," he looked down, smiling into his mug. His jawline looks like it could slice steel. "They only apologized for causing me to become independent at such a young age."

"Same here," I lower my head, staring even more deeply into his eyes. He looks over like I'd just cheered him up from a heartbreak, smiling gratefully. "My parents are almost always busy, so I spent most of my time alone and raising myself."

"What was your childhood like?" He asks me curiously. I lose myself in his eyes and allow myself to go into autopilot.

"Well I moved a lot growing up, so I never got the chance to get a best friend and all of my friends were temporary," I start. Amazement causes my jaw to drop because his smile didn't lessen despite me telling him that I didn't have friends growing up. Something ticks in me, my heart begins to race, and my breathing becomes deep and heavy. I look back into his eyes and a feeling of lightning erupts from my chest, it feels like a bolt of electricity is sparking between us. I lose my breath. What is happening to me? What is going on? I don't know and I don't care, I love this feeling, I never want this moment to end. "Um, I- I lost my train of thought. How about you?"

He smiles, dimples form in his cheeks and it feels like my heart is about to explode. "I've had the same friends my entire life, my grades were always average, I was never the top of anything, and I never did any extracurriculars because I was too busy with my siblings. I never minded it though, I love my siblings, sometimes they can even be far more interesting than any of the drama at school."

I start to howl from laughter, "That is amazingly true."

"Do you have any siblings?" He asks me, turning his head slightly to the side. "Or are you an only child?"

I twist my head a bit, "It's a bit complicated."

His smile makes me want to tell him about my entire life, he makes me want to never leave his side. Where has he been my entire life? "Feel free to explain, not like I have people to serve." He gestures to the empty yet comfortable cafe, the TV and music turned off at some point and I never noticed. I may have only just met him, but it feels like I've known him my entire life.

I giggle, "Well my parents adopted a lot of children, well, teenagers. They wanted to give them a good life and believed that the teenagers took priority since they may have gone through much more."

"That is so amazing of them!" Matt's face lights up, he looks proud of my parents despite never knowing them. "So why did they have a biological baby then? How many people did they adopt?"

"They adopted around twelve I think," I squint trying to remember the exact number but drawing a blank. His smile makes him look like an excited child that just met their hero or a superhero. "I'm not completely sure why they had me though, maybe they ran out of teenagers to adopt," I joke.

He chuckles, his smile makes my heart pound out of my chest. I bet if he looked close enough he would be able to see an outline of my heart just bumping. "You're parents sound like amazing people, how did all of the kids turn out?"

"One is working to become an actor, two are doctors, three are still in university, and the rest I'm not sure about," I respond, feeling proud of my parents as well. I guess his fiery joy must be contagious, even more than the Coronavirus. "Although, one is also working to follow in their footsteps and adopt children just like they did."

"Damn, they certainly know how to raise a child," Matt looks surprised.

"Are you the oldest out of all of your siblings?" I ask him. We both finish our hot chocolates and he goes behind the counter to make us some more.

From the other side of the room he shouts, "Second oldest, the oldest is ten years older than me."

"How?" I ask in amazement.

"My mother got pregnant when she was seventeen I think," he says, spraying extra whipped cream onto my hot chocolate and sprinkling some cinnamon on top. "They decided to keep it, my father's parents allowed my mother to move in with him since her parents kicked her out."

"What's he doing today?" I ask as he sets down my hot chocolate and sits back down.

"For work, I'm not sure, but I do know that he is living with his boyfriend somewhere," he shrugs. "The best memory I have of him was when he came home from school one day. He got suspended for getting into a fight after protecting a girl from getting picked on."

"What happened?" I ask, sipping my drink.

"It was a bad school, there were stuff like gangs and that," he mentions. "There was some guy hitting on her and she decided to ignore him and walk away. So the guy followed her, at that point my brother noticed the guy being suspicious and started following him. So, when the girl was exiting the school he cornered her. That's when my brother came in, grabbed the dude by the throat and threw him to the ground."

"How did your parents react?" I ask him, wiping some whipped cream over off of my hair. "Is the girl okay?"

"They were proud of him, told him to never change," Matt responded, a little bit of his smile disappeared but that makes sense. "Him in the girl ended up becoming friends and he ended up dating her brother, and they're still together to this day."

"Like any love story," I joke, trying to lighten up the tension.

He smiles, good my joke didn't upset him, "The love story they don't want you to know about."

"What's your opinion on a rowdy Christmas?" He suddenly asks me, checking his watch.

"It sounds interesting," I respond, trying to act like I don't already know what he's going to ask me. "Why do you ask?"

Matt shifts his entire body towards me, gazing lovingly into my eyes like his heart is in his hands, "I have had a pleasant time with you today, and I love talking to you."

I lose my breath for a second, my mouth becomes dry and I can feel my heart leave my chest and crawl into my hands, offering itself to him. "I- I feel the same way about you."

He takes a deep breath, his eyes twinkle in the moonlight, like they're about to transport me into a whole 'nother world. "Would you maybe like to spend the rest of Christmas with my family and I?" He checks his watch again, "I finish work soon, and well-"

"Yes," I respond. My racing heart is making it difficult to piece together an entire sentence, but I know what I want, and what I want is to spend more time with him.

His face lights up, brighter than the artificial fire that once was playing on the TV. He jumps up, full of joy, "My siblings are going to love you!" He's dancing and skipping all around the cafe, his joy bursting at the seams. "Just wait till my parents hear about how amazing you and your family is!"

He grabs my hand and pulls me into his arms and we start dancing to the sound of our footsteps and deep breaths. His heart is racing and in the heat of the moment I muster out an, "I love you."

He takes a deep breath and whispers into my ear, "I love you too."

Deathchill: Short Story

The room smells like tears and plastic. Bright colours cover the walls, multi-coloured carpets lay across the floor, blue and green tables and chairs spread throughout the room and small bookshelves of children's books stand in the corner of colour and positivity. The taste of lunchtimes juice lingers in my mouth, along with the smoked meat sandwich my dad made for me. The feeling of heat rests in my hands as I hold a flame in my palm. I've been able to use my powers for about two weeks now, and I've already gotten the hang of it. My other friends got theirs just a few days ago, and they were all so happy. Death, fire and cold, those are my powers. A few kids screamed at me and called me a demon when they found those out. But I didn't care. My true friends only thought of them as cool and amazing. Plus, one of my friends, Shi Hakaitit, also has a death power. Though, it makes more sense, he is an actual demon after all. I'm friends with two demons, Shi Hakaitit, his powers are death and teleportation, and Hakai Shinit, her powers are destruction and teleportation. Even though they're demons, they're still some of the nicest people I've ever met.

A thunderous crash along with a scream snaps me out of my day dream. Anne grabs my hand and pulls me towards it. She only has one power, and its mind reading. Some people call her weak since she doesn't have a fighting power, but I know she could take them all down in a fist fight, no problem. Shi and Hakai follow as we dash towards the noise.

Once we get there, we see a circle of children, around twenty. At first, it's not clear what's happening, but as we get closer we figure it out. We spot Samuel on the ground inside of the circle, bleeding and crying. His afro has loads of dirt and shards of glass in it and his mahogany skin is bruised with spots of blood. His clothes are ripped and destroyed; he went all out to look nice today. Well, he goes all out every day, but today was special. He was excited for show and tell, so he wanted to look his best. Samuel screams out in tears as the other kids stand there, laughing, and beating them.

My friends and I are frozen at the sight of him for a few seconds. Then Anne goes running up and pulling everyone to the ground, she shouts, "Leave Samuel alone!"

One of the kids grabs her hair and pulls her down. He has a glass power, so he's most likely the reason for the crash and all of the glass. He has red hair in the form of a mohawk, a black Nike muscle shirt and dark blue Nike Basketball shorts. He yells as he kicks her in the gut, "Shut up! You're weaker than him! You have a stupid power!"

That was the last straw for Shi and Hakai. There's a long history between those two demons, a history that would require an entire history book to explain. But something special that they both can do when put together, is transform. They join hands and transfer into their demon forms, they go from Shi and Hakai to Shi Soshite Hakai. They are the demons of death and destruction. Bits of Hakai's belly explodes, leaving holes all throughout her, but she isn't bleeding. Her eyes turn pure white, as white as a freshly fallen snow, and her hair grows longer, blowing through the wind. Shi's appearance completely changes. His adorable face is replaced by a black skull, with teeth as sharp as knives. Inside the skull is lava, flowing through his body, hotter than any flame I have yet to muster. His body is like armour made out of molten rock and a crown of fire lays atop his head.

Several kids run away screaming and calling us demons, others decide to stay and try to fight. I run over to Samuel and Anne while Shi Soshite Hakai covers me. "Are you guys okay?"

Anne coughs and wheezes but manages a nod, "Yeah, I'll be fine." I reach out my hands and they both grab it, "Let's kick their asses."

Samuel picks through his hair, still crying, "Why are they like this?" He whimpers.

I dust some dirt off his shoulders and smile comfortingly, "They're just jealous that you can turn into giant monsters." I rub some tears from his eyes and smile. "How about payback?" He chokes on his tears for a second, then nods. I smile wider, "Good."

We turn back around to see the red-headed kid shooting shards of glass at Shi Soshite Hakai. With every shot, Hakai explodes it back at him and it melts before it gets anywhere near Shi. Samuel's powers are take over and poison, sure, they may be strong powers, but Samuel still hasn't figured out how to make them work all the time.

Anne points to a girl standing nearby the red head, "She's about to send out a blast of water." I look back to the girl, she has long blonde hair and hot pink clothes. Her powers are water, ice, and weather.

"Got it," I quickly respond and bolt over to her. A deep black mist of death wraps itself down my forearm as I get closer and closer to her. Right before she sends out the blast, I slide on the ground and grab her leg. She wails in pain and collapses to the ground; tears quickly form in her eyes as I let go.

"Lexus!" Anne calls out and points to a pair not too far from me, they're nearby the slide on the playground. "The boy has fire and the girl has strength!"

"Samuel!" I yell as I hurry over to them. He perks his head up, covertly moping. "You get the girl; I'll get the guy!" He nods and rushes over. He takes the form of a dark grey wolf and pounces on the girl. I make my surroundings colder, weakening the boy's flame. I jump up and send a small ball of fire towards the boy, his clothes set slightly on fire and he runs away, screaming. I look over to see the girl's arm bleeding after Samuel bit her several times. I pull him off her and she scurries away.

Samuel transforms back, "Overdid it?"

I nod, "Just a little."

We turn around to see Anne in a fist fight with one of the boys. The boy's power is strength, she's using his power against him. The boy stomps on the ground and swings at her while she's catching her balance. Anne squats down, blocking the punch and head butts his gut. The boy is winded and drops to the ground, holding his stomach and crying. She looks over to us and smiles innocently. Samuel and I look at each other and giggle quietly.

Our attention switches over to Shi Soshite Hakai and the red-headed boy. He's growing apprehensive and has started sending out large amounts of glass. His breathing is frantic and he's sweating uncontrollably. He's running out of energy, and he's terrified of what Shi Soshite Hakai will do if he stops. Anne walks over to Samuel and I, none of us take our eyes off the fight. Shi starts moving his hands in a circle, forming an orb of deathly mist. Hakai does the same, but her orb is an explosive. The boy's face goes pale and he wets himself. The demons show an evil smirk and they throw the orbs towards the poor boy.

The boy attempts to run away, but he can't escape the explosions. The poor boy is engulfed in the flames of the explosions and screeches from the pain of the mist. A bitter taste appears in my mouth, like blood and fish, I hate fish.

"Stop that at once!" Our teacher screams, running out to the playground. Shi Soshite Hakai switch back to their human forms and attempt to hide their amusement. The teacher spawns in a blanket that can cancel powers and heal injuries, she tosses it over the boy and scowls at us as it heals the boy. "What's the meaning of this?"

All of once, we point at the boy under the blanket then at Samuel. The teacher gives a look of angered confusion and Anne decides to explain. "He and all of the other kids have been bullying him and I." She walks over to Samuel and points to his afro covered in dirt, glass and blood. "Look at him, his clothes are completely destroyed, he's covered in his own blood and who knows how much glass may be in his body right now."

The teacher stops to think for a second, analysing the bloody, destroyed playground. She lets out a frustrated sigh, "Fine, all of you go to the nurse. I understand that you were just protecting each other."

We do as she says without saying another word to each other. That is, until we got back into the school and out of hearing distance.

"That was so much fun," Hakai starts with a cheery smile on her face. She inspects Samuel's bloody body, "Sorry, I meant-"

"No it's fine," He smiles and quietly laughs to himself. "They got what they deserve." He looks at all of us, "Thank you guys, for having my back."

"Of course," Shi grins and picks sharps of glass out of his afro. "We'll always have each other's backs, forever."

"But did you guys see how he peed himself?" Anne asks, laughing along with her words.

We all join her in the laughter. "Yeah, he's going to be smelling terrible for a week!" I add.

We continue laughing and talking about all of the terrified children all of the way to the nurse's office. None of us regret a thing and our trust in each other grew astronomically ever since we had each other's backs. Almost nobody dared to mess with us after that, and we almost never left each other's side either. Anyone who did dare to fight us, got what they deserved.

Pyro Hero

"Help me set this fucking thing on fire!" Phyre shouts at the top of her lungs as she lunges another jerrycan onto the petit flame, which has no effect for an unknown reason.

"Typical aries," Shawna giggles as we continue to watch Phyre and Xipil struggle with our only way to get rid of the evidence. "Of course both of you go straight to burning things down."

"Such up with your stupid astro shit!" Xipil yells, glaring sidelong at Shawna.

"Somebody get the fucking gunpowder!" Phyre shouts, her huge biceps tighten as she tries to guard the baby flame from the sudden rainfall.

"We ran out!" I scream, watching our friendship go up in flames, unlike the paper. Pointing a hateful finger to Xipil's bomb sniffing dog, I relay to them, "Dumbo ate it all!"

"What!" Everyone else shouts in unison as Dumbo licks his paws, patches of gunpowder still linger on his fur.

Xipil lunges towards me, leaving Phyre on her own with the barely lit paper. His muscles glisten as he tightens a fist and snarls. "You fucking idiot, Isabella!" His fist collides with my face and my skin immediately starts to sting due to our wet skin. Shawna screeches, her high-pitched voice has definitely carried through the woods. But nobody else seems to care, Xipil is focused on me, and Phyre is focused on the flames.

Between breaths and a now bloody face, I exclaim, "But it's paper, shouldn't it set on fire?"

Xipil rolls his eyes and hits me once more before finally pushing up to his feet and examining his dog. "You idiot, it's wet, so of course it won't set on fire."

"But fire is hot-" I'm immediately silenced by Xipil throwing a ball of mud at my face.

"Classic Pisces," Shawna giggles while I wipe the disgusting mud off from my face. Phyre looks terrified, most likely from the combination of my bleeding face, Xipil's angered tension, Shawna's annoyingness and the flame getting weaker by the second.

"You're such a fucking idiot," Xipil mumbles, sounding upset and defeated.

"I'm not the dumb dog that ate the gunpowder!" I shout, gesturing a hand to Dumbo who's still licking some gunpowder off from his paws.

"How do I know," Xipil screams in my face, a vein bulging out from his neck. "If anything you might've eaten the gunpowder and blamed it on the dog!"

My mouth gapes open and I point to Dumbo's paws, "He's literally still eating the gunpowder! Look at his paws!"

"Maybe you just put some there so you can blame it on him!" Xipil rebuts me, I notice Phyre roll her eyes as she continues to try and protect the paper. "After all, it's not the first time you've blamed something on my dog!"

I gasp and there's a sudden sound of footsteps making their way towards us. Phyre appears over our shoulders and smacks us both upside the head, "Shut the fuck up and help me light the damn paper on fire already!"

"We literally put six whole jerry cans on it and it didn't do shit," Xipil reasoned, giving up almost immediately.

"Fuck, what do they make report cards out of these days?" I mumble, eyeing the now completely extinguished and soaked paper in Phyre's hands.

"Let's just go home," Shawna speaks in defeat as she lifts herself up. A patch of water leaves her butt soaking and impossible to miss. "I'm sure our punishment won't be that bad."

"What about our punishment for starting a fire in the woods?" Phyre asks, placing a hand on her hip and raising an eyebrow at her.

"Arson," Xipil shrugs like it's no big deal. I finally get up to my feet after remembering that nobody here is going to rush to help me. I wish Jonathan, or even better, if Tim was here. They wouldn't let anything bad happen to me. Gosh, Xipil is such an asshole, he's the worst brother ever.

"Let's just get going, best to get home before someone calls the police," Phyre throws her hands up in the air, the soaked paper folds and bends from the movement.

"But what about the report card?" I ask, pointing to the failing grade burning in Phyre's hand. The grade that will be getting us all sent away. It's going to be even worse if our parents find out about how we tried to get rid of the evidence.

"I'm sure that the water can easily destroy it," Shawna points towards the teary night sky.

"No way, the school knew how important this report card was to us," Phyre shakes her head, leaping over a patch of mud that can definitely steal a shoe. "I have no doubt that they went all out and made it waterproof."

"How about we just rip it?" I ask, gesturing to the flimsy sheet.

Phyre holds the sheet up in both her hands, gripping both corners tightly. Then, with a quick movement of her arms, she attempts to rip the paper. Xipil drops his head, cursing from frustration. I give him a look of confusion then look back to the paper, going wide eyed at the sight of the sheet still in one piece. The combined anger and tension of both Phyre and Xipil combined makes Dumbo whine and me shiver. Shawna holds back her laughter, she clearly wants to make another joke about them being Aries'.

"This is insane!" Phyre shouts, falling to her knees and making mud splash all over us. Shawna squeaks like a chihuahua from the impact and Xipil acts like he didn't even notice.

"Are we really that bad?" My voice adds emphasis to how defeated I feel as I flick bits of mud off of me.

"Well considering that one of our first ideas when it came to getting rid of evidence was to start a fire," Shawna starts, giving the two Aries' a shallow glare. "I'd guess so."

"Shut the fuck up," Xipil snarled and grabbed Dumbo's collar. He staggers through the soft, wet ground as the rest of us collect ourselves and follow him through the trees.

Other than grunting and Shawna weeping every few seconds, we're pretty much silent that entire walk. Phyre stomps her feet as she passes by me, which makes sense, her and Xipil are the most physically active here. So I bet that being behind me as a slow walker is probably pissing her off even further.

A soaked branch smacks me square in the face, making me wail from the stinging feeling and nobody even bothers to turn around and ask if I'm alright. I know for a fact that if I looked in a mirror then I'd definitely see a red slash, maybe even a little bit of blood.

We all get closer to the exit of the forest and Xipil stops, turning around to see the sad sight of his sister and two friends that he's about to lose. At this rate, none of us will be friends by the end of the night. Shawna's face is puffy from tears and Phyre is bright red from anger, she gets red a lot. Which is one of the things that I liked about her, especially since she was still pretty nice even when she was pissed.

"I'm going to miss you all," I mumble, though it was too quiet for anyone to hear me. I could barely even hear myself. Nobody acknowledges me, all eyes are on Xipil with his irritated expression and tight fists.

He clenches his teeth, "Stupid." My and Shawna's mouths gape wide open, but it seems that Phyre already knows what's on his mind. "You both are so fucking stupid, you're no help at all!" Phyre chooses to stay quiet, making sure to stay off of his bad side.

Then, something out of the ordinary for me happens. I get a burst of irritation and rage, I want to shout at him, lecture him, treat him how he's been treating me for years. I can easily hold myself back, but I like the feeling. It makes me feel powerful, like my anger could lead an entire army if I were to be pushed to my actual limits. My eyes burn, but not from tears, more of anger.

"Xipil," I clench my teeth just like him, ball my fist just like him, and match his fierce glare just like him. Except I won't lose control like he always does, I will destroy him and smile right after like the little angel I always get called.

He stares me down, making my blood boiling hotter than any pot. "What dumbass?" He speaks like his words are shooting a spear through my chest, but in reality, he's just equipping me with a weapon.

"W-" I start but immediately get cut off.

"Stop," Shawna stares at the muddy ground, clenching her fists and holding her eyes shut. Phyre and I shoot her a look, but Xipil keeps his deathly focus on me.

I can tell that he's trying to burn a hole into me, I can feel it. But I know it's not real, I'm safe. I always have to remind myself of that. I'm safe, I'm safe, I'm safe. He won't hurt me anymore than he always does, I am safe. He is my brother, I am used to it, I am strong, I can take it.

"Please just stop and calm down," I notice a tear fall out of her eyes, mixing in with the mud that's eating our shoes the longer we stand still.

Phyre marches over to her, trying not to fall in the mud and ruin the mood that she's about to bring to us. She wraps her arms around Shawna, prompting her to openly cry and speak words that none of us can understand. "It's alright," I can hear Phyre mutter, just loud enough past the pouring rain.

I take advantage of their moment and slog over to Xipil, who's still glaring at me with intense vexation. "You're a little bitch," I tell him, stopping just in front of me. I'm at the perfect spot to get punched in the face, so it would definitely be a better idea to not provoke him further. But what the hell? Fuck him.

"And you're not as innocent as you lead everyone to believe," His face lightens up a bit, it seems that we're on a mutual agreement.

I smile brightly and place my dirtied hands under my chin, giving that false smile of innocence. "I don't know whatever you're blabbering about."

"Blabbering?" He hollers in laughter. He may be making fun of me, but at least he's not beating me into the mud. The two girls look over to us, Shawna looks broken and terrified, but Phyre looks happy with a wet smile from the rain, I guess that I made the right choice.

He smacks my shoulders and continues to roar, his voice echoes through the trees, even louder than the rain. "So what's the plan then?" I ask, once the two girls join us closer to the border of trees. The wind whistles as we all take a moment to think. A truck drives by, just missing us with the splash of the puddle. Shawna jumps and both Phyre and Xipil chuckle, I stay quiet, like I always do.

"What about Shawna's older brother?" Phyre suggests and we all nod. Shawna's older brother, Matt, is the most destructive out of anyone we've ever met combined. Even more than Xipil and Phyre combined. He has been arrested more times than we can count, yet he still manages to be pretty nice. He even used his charisma to get out of being arrested several times before. He truly is a master of manipulation and deceit.

"Yeah that's an amazing idea," Xipil agrees with a tired tone. They both tend to compete a lot, mainly about who can do the most damage. Sometimes Phyre would even join in. It would always be a good show growing up, Shawna and I would always prepare drinks and snacks once we find out that they're about to challenge each other. She was always terrified at first when we were way younger, but she eventually gave in and decided to just enjoy it. We would even help them if there were to be a risk of getting in trouble. Xipil won a few times, but Matt definitely holds the majority.

"Yeah that is true," Shawna agrees and we follow each other out of the forest. "He is also a Scorpio, so that will help us even more."

Xipil looks sidelong at her with an annoyed look, "Shut up." Phyre giggles quietly.

After a few minutes of walking in silence, we get to an area where Matt normally hides out around this time, whether he's making little bombs or he's hooking up with a girl, he always comes here. It's a combination of a bridge, a few abandoned buildings and tall bushes and trees. Perfect for hiding and watching your surroundings. I wouldn't be surprised if he's an assassin and we never knew.

We all split up and search the area, making sure to keep a close eye on each other. We all turn our data on and start a video chat, that way it will be easiest for us to report anything. I enter one of the smallest buildings, it's rare to ever mind him in here since it's the least comfortable one and also the most revealing, but might as well check.

"Guys, I think I found him," Phyre, whispers into the call and I immediately see Xipil turn and run in her direction. Shawna and I do the same just a little less dramatic.

We all catch up with each other, I assume that Xipil went into the wrong building because he somehow got here after us. "Where is he?" He pants.

Phyre gestures to a shut door, there's a faint light shining bellow it and some music with way too many curse words playing at full blast. "It doesn't sound like he has a girl with him or anything."

"He might just be getting high," Shawna moves past us, keeping her hands clasped in front of her to hide her shaking. She knows that Matt won't do anything to hurt her, he's nothing like Xipil and me. But still, his reputation and actions are enough to make her a little anxious. She places her hand on the loose handle and shoves the door open.

I can't see much past all three of them, but I think he's sharpening one of his knives. Back when we were younger, Xipil and I were fascinated by his knife collection, now I just find it intimidating. However, Xipil is still fascinated from time-to-time.

A fresh cut is on the side of Matt's cheek and his hair is a mess. He's probably in a dangerous mood, yet he still smiles at us. A part of a song in his playlist takes over my thoughts for a second, 'Killers are nice, muggers are rough.'

"What happened?" I ask without thinking. Everyone else looks at me with confusion for a second but then I point to his cut and I notice Shawna shiver slightly. Though, I'm not positive if it's from fear or the mixture of cold and rain.

He gives me an assuring grin and says, "Don't worry about it." He gestures us inside with his knife then puts it down, we all pile in. "So what's up? What do you guys need?" Phyre holds up the soaken report card and Matt bursts into laughter. "I remember when I got one of those."

"Wait," Xipil's expression turns to astonishment. "You got one of these before?"

Matt raises an eyebrow and gestures around us, "No shit."

"So can you help us?" I ask with a hopeful tone, keeping my hands clasped in front of me like I'm begging him for assistance.

He snorts and pushes himself up to his feet, walking over to a closet with a loose door and sliding it open with great difficulty. Revealing several things that can cause terrible destruction in the wrong hands, which they are. A gas canister, chainsaw, guns, homemade bombs, and much more. He certainly has been busy.

We can all hear Shawna gulp, "Where did you get-"

"Don't worry about it," Matt grins again, this time it's a little more threatening. He then lifts up the chainsaw and places it in the middle of the room, doing the same with the jerry can immediately after.

"What are you going to do?" Phyre asks after handing Matt the paper.

He glances around the room a few times then shakes his head, "Best to do it outside." He peers over to Xipil and points to the jerry can, "Take it downstairs for me."

We all follow him back outside, Phyre notices Shawna shaking and gives her her coat. Xipil sets down the jerry can next to the chainsaw and turns to Matt, "What now?"

"Step back several feet," He warned us over his shoulder. Shawna sprinted towards one of the buildings and Phyre soon followed. Except Xipil just stood and stared at him, like he wanted an answer, or he was pissed because he thought he was being treated like a child.

"Xipil," I mutter, reaching for his sleeve.

He shakes me off and heads for the building that everyone is hiding in, a sour look upon his face. I shoot Matt a glance, trying to see if he's just as confused as I am. But I don't even see a hint of uncertainty, he looks like he knows exactly what's on Xipil's mind. But what is it? I don't understand these boys at all.

Matt raises an eyebrow at me and I realize that I've been staring. I take a gulp and tread towards the house, the spikes of rainfall nearly making me go blind.

I join the others crouching behind a cracked window as we watch Matt do whatever he's planning. The pouring rain makes it look like we're watching TV with static like when we were children. I miss being kids, the fights weren't as painful and we all were still innocent and happy.

Matt grabs the jerry can and starts pouring fuel onto the chainsaw, I immediately figure out what he's planning to do and I assume by the noises coming from the others that they've figured it out as well. He throws the now empty jerry can off to the side and takes a lighter out of his pocket. Covering the flame with his hand to protect it from the downpour. Then, with a quick flick of his wrist, he tosses the lighter onto the chainsaw and sprints in the other direction. Just managing to get out of the range of the explosion. After a few seconds of waiting for it to calm down a bit, Matt inches closer to the chainsaw and lifts it up, making sure to keep the flames away from his soaked clothes and fragile skin. He turns it on with only one swipe of the cord, it starts with a dangerous rattling as the blades pick up speed. We most likely don't have long before the fire gets into the gas tank of the chainsaw. Matt knows this, so he immediately faces the report card resting on the drenched ground and lowers the flaming chainsaw onto it. Immediately setting it on fire and ripping it to shreds in unison.

I'm sure that if we were closer to him then we'd be able to see some sort of psychotic smile or hear some maniac laughter, but for now we just assume that he's silent and helping us.

After a few minutes of Matt trying to extinguish the flame and us watching from afar, he finally signals us to come over. We get out from our spot and exit the building, treading over mud and potholes. I can feel Shawna trying to hide her fear of her brother, she's radiating an energy that makes him seem like he's even a danger to us. Which I know isn't true. We're Matt's most trusted allies, he'd never harm us. In fact, even when he was still in high school, he'd still protect us and beat up anybody who even whispered negatively about us.

We all stop in front of what's left of the ravaged report card, even if you tried you wouldn't be able to figure out a single letter on the paper. "I think it's dead," I suddenly mention. Matt snickers a bit and soon the others follow.

"Anything else?" He asks, eyeing our faces. Xipil is staring at him with amazement, like a child meeting an astronaut.

"Well-" Phyre almost starts but then the sound of a truck driving up sends us running to the houses.

We think that we've gotten inside before anyone saw us, but we still hide in a dark corner. Matt looks like he's analyzing the situation, thinking about the best way for all of us to escape.

"Xipil! Isabella! Dumbo!" The sound of our mother's voice is shouting into the wind.

"Shawna! Matt!" The voice of their father joins in.

Nobody is calling out for Phyre, I can see her face show heartbreak, but only for a moment.

Xipil holds Dumbo still and I try to keep him quiet and calm. "The fuck are we going to do?"

Then, something that made all of our attempts at freedom useless happened. Matt dropped his head to the ground like he just remembered something terrible. I gaze at him, hoping it's not as bad as it seems.

Matt finally speaks, he sounds absolutely defeated, "Report cards are also emailed to the parents."

Care For The Baby

The brick is covered in moss and crumbles when touched too harshly, reminds me of Steven.

"Hey! I heard that!" A high-pitched voice squeaks in the room next to me.

"And what did I tell you about passively reading people's minds?" The dark haired person next to me pushes their glasses up, the lights attached to them adjusting as they examine the old, dusty, thick books. "Especially Alex's."

"Hey," I retort, laughing.

"Just get back to examining, we need this book," Lennox dismisses us, brushing their finger along the spines.

"Correction," Steven steps back into the study, holding a fire poker stick for some reason. His long, dirty blond hair streaming over his shoulder. Leaves, sticks, and dirt still riddled throughout it from when he decided to run straight into the forest because he saw a squirrel that was too big for his liking. It's amazing that the scent of old people and dust in this building still manages to overpower his smug cologne. "We need it to get a hundred, not just in general."

"I still find it concerning how the teach wanted us to hike through a dark, empty forest and trespass in some old ass mansion just to find a dusty book," I mention taking the stick away from Steven. "Where did you get this anyway?"

He shrugs, "It was in the bathroom."

Did someone use it to plunge their ass?

"Ew Alex!" Steven cringes walking away from me and to the large wooden desk on the other side of the room. Papers are spread and piled across the entire thing, coffee stained files overflowing with documents.

"Stop reading Alex's mind!" Lennox shouts, their voice echoing throughout the building.

"Don't tell me what to do," Steven pouts, crossing his arms and spinning around in the office chair.

We continue searching in silence, Steven checking the drawers, Lennox examining the books, and myself wandering around. Being the most helpful of course. A breeze brushes my shoulders and I shake, stopping to put on my hoodie. My fingers brush along the side of a sofa, thick layers of dust and grime leaving a residue on my hands. But then my movement stops, and I listen, shutting out the motions of my groupmates. Something doesn't feel right.

"Alex, I didn't take you for the paranoid type," Steven voices from the room over. Except, that's not the room he was in, and I didn't see nor hear him switch rooms. Two floors up, something drops and the soft cry of a baby begins to ring in my ears.

"Alex, we're busy over here, can you go see what happened?" Lennox's voice asks, except, just like with Steven, it's not in the right place. I can't use my power, this building does smell like old, yes, but there's also a hint of gasoline. There's no way we can risk an explosion.

Rushing back to the study where my group mates were, the door shuts, slamming on my face. Steven screams, "Alex!"

"Steven! Lennox!" I cry, banging on the door and twisting on the rusted handle. The knob falls, dropping to the ground with an echoing bang. It rolls over to the staircase, each thud being a pound beating at my growing headache. My body burns, but I breathe and focus on the chilliness of the mansion.

"Alex, stay calm!" Lennox shouts and the door shakes followed by Steven grunting.

They continue screaming and ramming into the door, but the noises fade. Footsteps coming down the stairs force my ears to twitch, the crying like a melody entrancing my consciousness. My vision begins to tunnel as my body slowly turns, watching as the stairs shake and dust drops from the vibrations. Grey bare feet catch my sight from the top of the stairs and a hush takes over the mansion. The lights go black and I give in, no longer caring about the consequences.

I hold my hands out in front of me and set them aflame, dully illuminating my surroundings, sparks flashing in the air. My flames may be hot, but my body freezes upon seeing them. My groupmates, bodies grey and eyes lifeless, stand in front of me, faces twisted upwards like pained smiles.

As their mouths move, it sounds as though multiple bones are cracking. With a pneumonia ridden exhale, they speak in screeches that make my ears bleed, "You should have checked on the baby."

Indecent Breaths of Nature

The wind blows, making sharp knives of liquid flow horizontally, hitting and stabbing anything and everything that dares to go out on such a dark, chilly night. The trees have turned a dark brown, moist from the painful shots of water, yet hydrated and rejuvenated in a sense. Whistling plays a chorus through the leaves along with the pelting against the Earth, from bass to alto, every plant and animal contributes to the orchestra of Gaia. Petrichor fills the air, swirling with the gusts, clinging onto any material it possibly can. Like it's holding onto its temporary existence as much as it can, as tight and as long as it can. But it will not last. Nothing lasts in this world. Lakes have dried up. Forests have disappeared. Animals have murdered and eaten one another. Hell, even the sun is temporary, for short term and long term. Though this brief storm counts as short term, for some creatures, it feels as though it has lasted years. Years of the fear and suffering every being is expected to go through all because "that's just life." Even long after one completes their life cycle and falls into the Earth just like the little drops of rain, their spirits will still remain. Suffering. Watching. Waiting. Waiting for the storm to come to an end. Watching as others fall. Suffering through the cold and damp winds that sing into their souls. The wind calms for just a moment, and someone, somewhere, may have been able to see the beauty of the rain, the mist that creates the bright sparkling rainbows. But it will all be shut out again. The wind will always rage on. Growing stronger with the rain.

Sky Guardians

A sudden chill makes my entire body shake, leaving just as fast as it came. The teacher in front of my class continues to talk about resumes and how we're never going to amount to anything. Classic. I don't even get why people like that even teach, they clearly don't like their job anymore. Besides, it's not like they can't just go back to school or switch career paths. There's plenty of jobs that you can go to that don't require any money. Like McDonalds, which is what this teacher says the majority of the class will be working in for the rest of our lives. A girl not too far from me sprays her perfume, pumpkin spice promptly suffocates me and hastily spreads to the others. As I cough the chemicals get onto my tongue, making my mouth numb and my anger rise.

The desk squeaks noisily as I rise up to my feet, gripping the wood-metal combination tightly in between my fingers. The metal is cold and wood warm, leaving the portions of my hands feel the exact same for a few seconds after I let go.

"What?" The girl asks with a cocky scowl. Her hair couldn't be any less fake, the black is clearly a wig and she didn't even angle it all that well either, you can clearly see her real brown hair underneath. Her makeup is too cakey as well, and her concealer is several shades too dark for her natural skin colour. Her neck stands out far more than her face, you can clearly see where she completely gave up on blending it all in.

Taking a deep breath, I decide to go the kind route, "Can you please stop spraying your perfume in the middle of class? It's very irritating, disruptive, and makes me feel sick."

"Ew, no you creep, get away from me," She angles her perfume bottle at me and sprays it directly on my face, luckily not getting it in my eyes.

That's it. Fuck this bitch, I'm going to kick her ass. "Listen here you fucking whore, I don't know if you know this or not but changing your appearance won't make you good looking, especially if you can't even do it properly."

"Excuse me?" The girl's jaw drops and the entire class murmurs amongst themselves.

"Fedrick Loosenburg, sit back down right now or go to the office!" The teacher shouts loud enough to make everyone jump. The more dainty students subtly begin to cry, only some of them having a friend to comfort them.

But I don't relent, I won't relent. This girl has been a narcissistic bitch ever since I met her last year in ninth grade. Everytime this girl walked into one of my classes, everyone instantly knew that it was going to be a nightmare. "It seems that the constant use of perfume has ruined your brain, and with it, your hearing. So I will repeat myself once more." Clapping between each of the words, I shout in her face. "You. Are. Not. Hot."

The girl gasps and sprays me once more with her perfume. "You are a misogynistic asshole! No wonder no girl will ever love you!"

"And with a body, face, and personality like yours," I hesitate for a moment, wondering if I should really go through with it. But oh well, not like it matters anyway. "No guy will ever truly love you."

"Fedrick, you will never live up to anything if you go around treating girls like that!" The teacher roars, his voice loud enough to even make the next-door teacher come over to check things out.

"Just you wait!" I start, clenching my fists by my side, ignoring all of the eyes and cameras locked on me. "I will amount to everything and achieve even the highest of goals!"

"Oh, and what might that be?" The teacher smirks, raising an eyebrow towards me.

I'm at a loss for words, not thinking this through whatsoever. What even is the highest level of goals? Prime Minister? No, even complete idiots can become that if they're lucky enough. Come on, dumbass, think, what is the highest of goals? What does a majority of the population want to be but a majority of them fail?

"That's what I thought," The teacher scoffs at me, rolling his eyes like he's being relatable by picking on me.

"I will become a sky guardian!" I shout, declaring it to possibly the entire school. The class is silent for a moment, the teacher goes to respond but I promptly cut him off, making my throat sore with all of the shouting. "Just you wait! I will become a sky guardian and prove to you that I can and will achieve the highest of goals!"

"Is that so?" The teacher continues to mock me, but the rest of the class remains silent as they gaze at me in sad awe. They don't think I'll make it. But I will. I'm too stubborn to lose. "Well, then I look forward to seeing you on the streets or even at the McDonalds after I ask you for extra sauce."

♘ ♘ ♘

The sky is freezing as the clouds fly past, air flowing through my long battle braids. The wind blows in my ears, the only other thing I'm able to hear is the neighing of my trusty alicorn and the occasional reports of my army. Its bright gold mane reflects beautifully under the high sun, and its clean white coat shimmers as we ride through the clouds. The diamond armour that has recently been gifted to me seems to be fitting quite well, it isn't distracting my steed and it's the most protective level of armour that has ever been created so far.

"Sir Loosenburg," The voice of one of my comrades shouts over my headset.

"Yes, private?" I shout back, now raising my guard back up to when I first heard the news and was sent out to defend.

"We are now in position and the targets are in sight," The voice continues to shout, but it's slowly becoming more concerning, like they're scared of something.

"Is something the matter, private?" I ask, pulling back on the reins and signalling my squad to stop.

"Yes, we have a clear view of them," The private reports and my gut sinks. It's possible that his squad has been taken hostage by whatever has chosen to attack our planet this time around. "We believe that it may be a code neon."

"Squads A and F, rendezvous with squad D and make your way to squad Y!" I shout the orders and the clouds around us begin moving with due haste. Pegasi soar in and out of view at fascinating speeds, rushing towards squad Y in an attempt to save them from whatever may be happening.

I turn my alicorn to face the direction of squad Y and gesture to my squad to follow suit. As we blast through the sky, one of my comrades works to keep up next to me, "Sir, what about the plan?"

"We are going against ancient mutant creatures that have destroyed entire cities and multiply at insane speeds," I respond slowly and calmly, trying my best to keep a level head. "Right now it would be best to assist the squad that is currently under attack since they are the closest to the danger."

"But-"

"If the boss has something against what I'm ordering then you can direct her to me, otherwise, stick to the plan!" I shout, trying to distract the others away from my shaking hands by raising my voice.

"Alright sir," The private falls back with the rest of the squad as we continue to speed forward.

The clouds disappear behind us as we cross the threshold and gaze upon the open sky. It's completely empty and oddly quiet. None of the squads are in sight, and there's not even a hint of our foes' presence. I raise my fist into the air, signalling my squad to stop.

The area is dead silent, not even a breeze is strong enough to grab our attention. Stroking my steeds mane, we listen closely to even the tiniest shift in our surroundings. Neither the alicorn nor the pegasi are showing any signs of something being wrong. It's not wise to call in either since we'll be making ourselves known and put everyone in danger. Is it possible that we went to the wrong location? No, never. Never in my twenty years of being the second strongest guardian in the sky have I ever made such a mistake. So is it possible that squad Y went to the wrong location? But then that doesn't explain why squads A, F, and D aren't present.

"Sergeant Major!" A voice shouts in warning. Before I'm even completely able to register it, I'm sent flying backwards. Free-falling through the air, searching for my steed through the upcoming swarms of clouds.

A barely noticeable neigh makes its way into my ears, followed by the screams of my comrades. One of the clouds begins to turn, large white tentacles reaching out of its top. A pug-like face with deep red, demonic eyes appears on the cloud. One after another, clouds turn to face me as I continue to plummet down to my probable death. Another neigh makes its way into my ears, and finally, my beautiful alicorn flies completely through one of the clouds, causing a liquid of some sort to pour out of it. I reach out a hand, placing all of my trust into my steed like I have been ever since I taught it to fly.

The alicorn's mane touches my hand and I grip onto it tightly, flipping myself over and landing directly on my steed's back. We hover mid-air for a moment as I analyze the situation, promptly realizing that what we thought were clouds, was actually the enemy surrounding us. I'm assuming that their ugly pug faces opened up and ate all of the squads as they were flying through. But then again, we were flying through clouds as well, so that makes this whole thing even more dangerous since it's going to take an extra second to depict clouds from weird squid pug cloud monsters.

"Is anybody still alive out there?" I shout out, keeping a close eye on my surroundings. The ground is a little visible below me, my old high school just barely in sight. Huh, I guess I achieved even higher than the highest of goals, instead of just being a sky guardian, I lead my own army of sky guardians. An army that I failed to protect from some ancient creatures. Now it's possible that every last one of them may be dead, all because of my incompetence. I should've told everyone to retreat, at least then we'd still have a few squads alive.

A large, white tentacle comes flying towards me, the alicorn shooting forward and out of the way just in time. As we spin around we're met eye-to-eye with the horrendous pug face. Blood drips out of its eyes and mouth, turning to vapour before it even reaches the ground. I see, so eating living things can help them stay alive, and the blood consumed can make them bigger.

"Sergeant Major, this is Colonel Jasper, what is your current situation?" A voice suddenly speaks over my headset.

"From what I know, all squads have been wiped out and I'm the last one standing," I explain, watching the pug raise closely and refusing to blink. "I am requesting backup and for permission to use the alicorn horn."

There's a moment of silence on the line, and the pug eyes begin to rise higher. "Permission granted, backup is on the way."

I tap the side of my steed's neck and whisper softly, "Come on, Magnon, it's time to go all out."

There's a brief neigh, and the horn begins to shine golden, red sparkles sprinkling down and disappearing. The tip of the horn grows brighter and brighter, eventually becoming pure white. A beam starts to shoot out from the horn, completely impaling the cloud and all else around it. Carefully, I slip on some goggles and direct Magnon towards the rest of the clouds in the sky, watching in awe as each and every one of them is sliced in half, their odd goo floating upwards towards space. The bodies of my comrades are covered in goop as they plummet back to the Earth, both them and their steeds completely unconscious. The backup will get to them, no worries.

"Hold your fire!" A voice plays over my headset once more, this time it's feminine, must be the highest rank.

Patting Magnon's neck once more, I whisper, "You did a good job today, buddy. Time to rest." The beams of light reach back into the horn and it slowly becomes dull once more. We begin plummeting back to the Earth once more together. Using up so much power has always caused my alicorn to faint. "So why did you want me to stop?" I ask, holding onto my steed tightly as our speed picks up and our armour begins to burn.

"We need to keep the rest for research, we already have people containing the live ones," My boss explains professionally. "And you are about to be caught in just a few seconds."

After about five seconds we land on a large net, my comrades being checked up on by field medics and having the goop removed. I refuse to let go of my steed, laying there next to it and petting it gently waiting for them to slowly lower us back to the ground.

"I thought we were all goners," I chuckle, talking to myself. Pointing a middle finger towards my old I school, I whisper, "Suck it, Mr. McCabe!"

The Guidance of Numuin

"The fairies aren't as far away as you might think," Spoke an old yet wise voice. It echoes through the trees, making me feel protected, like someone is watching over me. But I know that is not the case, for I have done so much wrong, I am unworthy of protection. Of guidance.

"I don't know what you mean by that," I exclaim speaking only to the trees, since the vessel of such a wise voice is currently imperceptible.

A cool breeze flows past my shoulders, causing my bits of bare skin to shiver. An empty feeling grows within me, the breeze makes me feel as though a loved one has left me. But there's no way that's possible, I have been completely alone for what feels like hundreds of lifetimes. Nobody can leave my life if they're never in it in the first place.

"You truly believe that?" A small, squeaky voice behind me questions me.

I head snaps over to where the voice was present, but nothing is in sight. "Who said that?"

"Oh I see," The voice squeaks again, still behind me.

"And I don't, where are you?" I begin to spin in circles, searching for where the voice is coming from, and shouting into the wind.

A sweet scent blows past my nose, making me feel like a child, or a young adult in love. A second later, I'm in a dark apartment. It's nice, a little fancy even. There's a huge flat screen TV mounted to a wall with a large, expensive looking couch resting in front of it. Two vast windows are on either side, opening up to a beautiful terrace overlooking an excitingly well lit city. I begin to look around, there's a large kitchen filled to the brim with expensive and- depending on one's opinion- useless appliances. Such as a coffee machine that can make its own latte art, and a food processor.

"Where am I?" I mumble as I make my way down a hall.

There's four doors in this hall, the closest one being a bathroom. Glancing into the room and immediately stopping in my tracks, I see a toilet with what might as well be hundreds of buttons on it. It's the same for the shower and the sink. There's even an intricate towel heating rack thing on the wall.

"Why am I here?" I roll my eyes at the expensive bathroom and move on down the hall.

The second door seems to be a laundry room filled with costly clothes and even more pricey equipment. I catch a glance of a gown, sparkling and nearly jaw dropping with it's beauty. Next to it, a suit that's no less than the gown. Those two next to each other just makes the other seem even more ravishing.

"Who's place is this?" I step out of the laundry and go to check out the third door.

This one seems a little off. All of the other doors have a basic handle and wooden design. But this one has a cold and silver handle with a door that must be made out of steel. Based on the exterior design alone, this room must be filled to the brim with armor and swords.

Taking a breath of the no longer sweet, but still lonesome air, I take hold of the handle and open the door. I was immediately proven wrong when Isaw that it was just a guest bedroom of some sort. There's an entire wall for video games and systems, it looks like there's generations worth of electronics here. The bed across from it appears that it must cost more than that entire wall combined. I wouldn't be surprised if it has massage features too.

I couldn't bear to check out the rest of the room, and there was a lot more of it as well. I rush out of it, slamming the door behind me. "What has gotten into me?" I whisper as I hold my hand up to my rushing heart.

After a few minutes of leaning against the extravagant door and catching my breath, I push back to my feet and trudge over to the last room. My feet get more and more heavy with every step, like I'm marching through fields of thick mud during a rainstorm.

Stopping outside of the last room, something metallic appears in my mouth. "Blood? No." It turns hard, like I'm biting down on an actual block of metal. Choosing to ignore, I enter the final room.

I almost scream at the sight of so many people, but then notice that it's a room full of mirrors. I look… off. I don't look like the me I always see. I look like I've merged with someone else. My eyes look gray like I haven't slept in years, and everything about me is a mess, from my hair to my clothes. My face is even a bit puffy, like I've been crying nonstop.

"Who am I?" I pick at my face in front of one mirror as I ask myself this. "Who are you?"

I'm not sure if I was expecting a response or not, but I never got one.

There's a thunderous crash followed by blood-curdling screams coming from the kitchen. Before I know it, all of the mirrors have cracked and glass falls all around the room. Almost like crystals raining from the sky, or the tears of the fairies that I've been told about my entire life.

Wait. Told about? Who could've possibly told me this stuff if I never had anyone in my life? "How did I get here? How do I get back? How do I know this?"

The traumatizing sound of stomping rushes towards the room I am being rained on by glass in. It makes my heart rush. Makes my blood boil and freeze millions of times over. Makes me feel like I'm having a flashback without the visions.

The steps stop just outside of the door and a furious, heavy hand grabs the doorknob. Without thinking I scream louder than the crashing of the glass, "Get me out of here!"

The door bursts open and I'm out. It's raining now. It's heavy, almost like liquid crystals. I cough up blood but I have no clue why. I don't want to move, I don't want to breathe. If I stay still then they'll think that I'm asleep and they won't hear me.

Wait. What am I talking about? Nobody could possibly hurt me if I never had anybody.

"What's going on?" I ask through thick breaths. The forest is more visible once again. It must be nearing day because the trees seem a bit brighter. Like bits of light are peaking through.

"You have forgotten," The wise voice speaks again. Though, this time it brings me no comfort, it only causes me to become angry. "More of you were forced to forget."

"Forgotten what?" I shout at the trees. "Why can't I see you? What just happened?"

"Trauma," The wise voice speaks again.

"How could I possibly have trauma?" I question the voice, trying to hold back my anger. "I never had a life that can possibly give me it!"

Something strange happens. The light shining through the trees begins to move at a rapid pace, zooming through the trees and spinning around me like a tornado of beauty. High pitched, squeaky voices all talk together as they join each other above me in their circle of sparkles.

A pit of fear grows within me as I jump to my feet and run in an attempt to escape it. But it follows me, thousands of different colours chase me through the trees. There is no escape. I have wished for this since I was a child, but now that I'm experiencing it, I don't want it. I'm being chased by fairies. What they want to do with me is a mystery. Whether I die tonight or not will soon be decided.

Then, a fate deciding misstep happens. I trip or a root and land face first in the mud. Every last bit of darkness disintegrates as I'm consumed by the light. Shutting my eyes, I accept my fate. It's not like anybody will miss me. I never had anyone. Nobody even knows that I've ever existed.

"Shut up," A fierce voice orders me. I'm standing now, and am completely clean. My eyes are still shut, I'm deciding if I should even open them or not. The deep, feminine voice sighs heavily, "Open your eyes."

I do as she says, slowly opening them and taking in my surroundings. We're in a completely black room with no source of lighting, yet we can still see each other perfectly. She has a tough, tomboy style. She looks strong, proud, always ready for anything. I wish I could be her, she looks amazing. Too bad I'm stuck with this sack of nothing.

The girl rolls her eyes, "Are you done yet?"

I give her a gaze of confusion and hurt. Why does it matter to me what she says or even does? I don't know her, she is nothing to me, just like how I'm nothing to her.

"Who are you?" I ask her, giving her a look of awe.

"Too bad you can't remember," She mumbles and picks at her nails. "I understand though."

"Understand what?" I twitch slightly, glaring at her. I already know what she's going to say. She understands me and what I'm feeling. I heard it all the time.

Wait. No I didn't. How-

"Trauma can cause memory loss," The girl responds, still focused on her nails. "The fairies will help you remember."

"Shut up," I clench my fists, digging my fingers into my palms.

The girl exhales a laugh and a mirror appears in front of me. Not cracked or anything, though it still looks pretty basic. I give her one last glare then look into the mirror. I look different. Not like me from earlier. My face looks healthy, my skin is flawless and my clothes look new. My hair isn't a mess and I don't look weak. I look happy despite the fact that I'm frowning.

"I don't want to remember," I say out of nowhere. I don't even know where it came from. I wasn't thinking that at all. "Wait, no."

The girl smiles and nods, "Then instead the fairies will help you find your way out."

The girl raises a hand but I shout, "Wait!" She stops. "How did I get here? Like into the forest?"

"You're not in a forest."

The light disappears around me but one still straggles nearby. It's light blue, like a water or wind fairy. How do I know this? I'm still in the forest though. What was that girl talking about? I'm clearly in a forest.

The light assumes a shape on my shoulder, it's beautiful. The fairy is wearing a long, light blue dress with a crown that seems to be forged from the stars. It's wings are an even lighter blue with it's nerves sparkling a rainbow. It's hair is a long and flowy brown.

"W-what's your name?" I stutter as I admire the fairy.

The fairy attempts to speak but then stops itself. It flies off of my shoulder and begins to write in the air, light blue sparkles follow it's glorious wings. Once the fairy finishes it rests back on my shoulder and I read out it's spelling.

"Numuin." The fairy nods. "Alright, Numuin, what are we doing?" Numuin points in a random direction and without any questions I go that way. "Alright then."

We walk for what feels like nearly an hour and I still see no change in location, not even a hint of a clearing. It's aggravating really. Just then, a mosquito swoops down and bites my neck, I smack it, blood squirts all over my hand.

"I hate this place!" I shout, Numuin flinches at my anger. I'm assuming that me yelling caused more mosquitoes to get pissed off because only moments later I'm getting swarmed. I scream as I run away, jumping over large roots and getting whipped by wet branches, causing my skin to appear red with scars. Numuin seems fed up with me for an unknown reason, I know this due to the fact that I can hear her heavily sigh in my ears. Why isn't she helping me? Isn't she supposed to be guiding me out of this hell hole?

Once again, I trip and fall over a large root, landing face first into the mud. Numuin leapt off my shoulder before I fell, so she didn't even get splattered. My anger rises inside of me like a flame growing to become a tornado of fire. The mosquitoes begin to attack, just causing me to lose my cool even more.

Before I get inhaled by the horrible, demonic creatures of hatred and blood, a light blue beam flashes past me, causing them all to scramble away. As I lift my mucky face out of the drowning mud, I catch sight of Numuin shining like a star from the furthest ends of space. It's almost inspiring really. It makes me feel just a little lighter inside.

Just then, the sky lightens up and streaks of light reach through the trees. This time I'm positive that they aren't fairies either. It truly is an amazing sight, and as fast as my anger came it has now also disappeared.

Slowly, I lift myself back to my feet. Numuin brings me a large leaf to wipe the mud off of my face. I accept it with a smile and it does an amazing job at clearing up the mud.

Tossing it back to the ground, I raise my palm and allow Numuin to land in it, "What just happened?"

"Well," Numuin squeaks and my eyes widen from shock.

"You can talk?" I try to keep my voice down, I don't want to ruin her hearing by speaking too loudly.

Numuin smiles wide, "You can finally understand me?"

"Is that why you drew your name instead of speaking it earlier?" I feel a wave of joy and energy stream through every inch of my body. Like it's growing plants within my nerves.

Numuin nods, her wings seem to sparkle even brighter with the increasing light. "You must be at a certain level in life to be able to understand us."

"What does that mean?" We begin walking once more, I keep her well positioned in my palm, making sure not to move my hands too much.

"My name means growth," She starts explaining as I carefully step over a bunch of large roots. It's much easier to see them now that it's brighter. "In order for you to understand me, you must grow as a person. Which you have managed to achieve."

"I guess that makes sense," I mumble, trying to wrap my brain around everything. "How much longer until we find our way out?"

"That's a process," Numuin giggles, providing me with no help whatsoever. I roll my eyes and my surroundings begin to grow dimmer. Her voice is barely audible when she says, "If you keep that up then you won't be able to understand me again."

"Whatever," I grumble and drop the hand she was resting on. She floats next to me as we continue to make our wave through the vast and towering trees. I can tell that she is a mixture of fed up and worried about me.

Eventually it becomes pitch black once more like it's midnight in winter, the only light is emitting off of Numuins wings and that's not even enough for me to see anything. We stop outside of a large, open tree. The kind with a trunk that a few people can fit inside of. Numuin flies over to it and signals me to join her. I guess that we'll be resting here for now.

I crouch inside of the trunk, doing my bed to ignore the spiders, beetles and other horrifying pests. Though they don't seem to be ignoring me. The more I think about how much I hate them, the more they come to bother me. It's like an annoying little sister.

The temperature grows chilly as my heart slows from the cease of movement and activity. I wrap my arms around my waste and lay down in hopes that my own bodily temperature will keep me warm enough. But it doesn't last long till I begin to see my own struggled and jagged breaths. Glancing over to Numuin, I see her watching me, waiting, hoping for me to lighten up a bit more.

Now I see. The worse I feel, the more hell of an experience this will be. But I can't help if I'm short tempered. It's not like breathing exercises or meditation will help me. That shit never works.

I notice my hair begin to frost from the cold and my ears feel as though they will fall off. I sniff the air, it smells like a winter morning, the kind that should have snow everywhere. I wouldn't be surprised if it started to snow. My nose runs and I cough for a good minute, I must be coming down with something. I'll probably be dead before I ever even get near to escaping this forest.

Numuin comes out of nowhere and grabs my face with her little hands, looking a little desperate. She's squeaking loudly but I have a feeling that I know what she's saying. She's begging me to stop thinking like that.

"How am I supposed to calm down if things just keep getting worse?" I ask her, with genuine concern for how everything will turn out.

She lets go of me and writes something in the air. Sadly, her glorious sparkles provide me with no warmth whatsoever. She finishes writing and lands back in front of me. She spelt out, 'Look Positives.'

"Look for the positives?" I give her a questioning glance. She nods frantically. "I don't see anything positive though, and I wouldn't really say that I'm still alive is a positive at this moment." I begin to cough repeatedly, tasting a hint of blood as I struggle to breath. My gut cramps up as I hold it tighter, wincing in pain.

Numuin grabs my face once more, and slaps me. It doesn't hurt or anything, someone of her size couldn't damage me. But it does leave me shocked, and for a moment- and only a moment- the pain disappears.

"It's all in my head," I groan, clenching my teeth as the pain increases and decreases like a rollercoaster in the clouds. I wonder what it would be like to feel a cloud. Would it be thick, or would my hands pass through it as easily as air?

The pain lightens.

Damn, now I want some cotton candy. I wonder if cotton candy would melt if it were to touch a cloud like it does when it touches water. I lick my lips, noticing that they're dry. I could really go for a nice, icy cold glass of water right now. Oooh or maybe a calming cup of jasmine tea. Jasmine is my favourite.

The pain is little to none by the time I exit my fantasy. Food is always a good go to when you need a distraction. Chuckling, I lift myself up. Numuin is staring at me with pure astonishment as our surroundings warm up and rays of light begin to peak through once more.

"How did you?" Numuin questions me, looking all around like we're just teleported somehow.

"Food," I immediately respond. We both laugh loudly and everything brightens like it's midday.

"That is a good starting point," She smiles and peaks outside of the tree trunk. "Though you'll need to think of more powerful positive thoughts as we continue to walk."

"Obviously," I chuckle and exit the trunk. She gets back on my shoulder and I admire our surroundings as I skip and leap or roots and small streams. It's a calm and cozy morning, the kind that will make you want to be outside all day.

"I think you are ready for the next step," Numuin randomly says as I admire a patch of glorious flowers. "I have to warn you though, it will be painful."

I almost question her for what she means by that but then think of a better response. With an expression of eagerness I cheer, "Bring it on!"

She smiles even wider, "Alright then. Follow me." I do as she says. After almost no time of walking, we found a cave. Though it doesn't seem like any normal kind of cave. Before we enter it I can already see drawings on the walls, nothing like cave paintings of people hunting, but more of the kinds of drawing a child would make.

As we enter, I notice an area of a variety of flowers directly in the center of the cave. They appear healthy and lively despite being in the middle of a dark cave. "What am I supposed to do?"

Numuin shrugs, "I don't know, figure it out."

Now I understand why she provides so little context, it's hardly growth and improvement if you're always given the answers. As I make my way over to the flowers, I notice them grow even more healthy.

I sit in the middle of them, crossing my legs and hoping that I didn't kill them. Shutting my eyes, I'm immediately transported to another world. I didn't even need to take a breath, amazing.

It's dark. I hear cars honking and driving through puddles not too far from where I stand. As I take in my surroundings, I realize that I am in the middle of an alleyway. It smells of piss and trash, it nearly makes me gag. I already want to leave, I already hate it here. I can feel wet cobblestone under my feet and my drenched hair creates knots around my shoulders. Glancing down, I notice that I'm missing a sandal. My mouth tastes off, like I've been crying and my tears have been falling onto my tongue as I wept. Finally, I hear shouting in the distance. It's a man and a woman. The woman cries and screams for help as the man shouts at her to shut up.

Running towards the commotion, I see the man holding the woman's hair with one hand and wacking her with my sandal in with the other. They're faces are blurred, blanked out by a black censorship bar.

The woman glances over at me and screams, "Alex, run away! Get help!"

The man throws her to the ground, shouting, "Shut up, bitch!" He begins to stomp his way towards me and I freeze up. My nerves turn to ice and I collapse onto the freezing wet stone. "Get over here!" The man shouts once more only a step away from me and everything turns dark.

I'm back in the cave but my heart is racing. I want to scream, cry, and throw up. I want to be safe, I'm not safe. I'm never safe. I don't deserve safety. I'm weak and useless. I can't do anything right.

The outside has become night once more and I can see Numuin worriedly watching me as I lose control. Why isn't she trying to help me? Right, growth. Fucking growth. I hate this. I hate everything just like how everything hates me.

Also, who is Alex? Am I Alex? Who was that woman? Was that supposed to be my mother? No, there's no way. I never had a mother. I never had anyone. But if she is, then who is that man? Is he- I sure hope not, but is he my father? What was happening? If that was me then how old was I in that time? Right, I need to think positive thoughts. I can slowly figure this out as we go, but for now, I need a distraction. But what happened after everything went dark? Oh god, I don't want to think about that. No good lies in the darkness.

"Hello? Can you still understand me?" Numuin appears right in front of me and I give her a tearful nod. "Good, you really are growing." She looks me up and down, I'm sure that I look hideous right now with my ugly crying. "I know it's painful, but I know that you will grow past it. I believe in you."

Her words feel empty to me, but I know she really does care. I need to focus, I need to get out of this forest. I wonder what it would be like to live in a cabin in the woods. Waking up every morning to the beautifully shining sun, going out to the lake and swimming everyday and night. Climbing trees and reading books in them. Having barbecues with friends over. I wonder what it would be like to have friends. Sleep overs and laughter. Going to the movies together, having lunch together, hanging out in the neighbourhood together. The very thought of it all makes me cry, but not the tears I've been crying for what feels like my entire life, but tears of joy and hopefulness. I'm sure that if I had friends, no. Once I get friends, they will be able to cheer me up whenever I cry those tears of sadness again. If we were both sad at the same time then we will be able to cry together, only increasing our bond.

It's day out again once I finally completely calm myself down. I feel truly happier, I feel like I'm looking forward to getting out of this forest. I'm going to miss Numuin, but I'm sure she will enjoy going back home to the other fairies as well once she's finished guiding me.

"Ready to go?" She asks once she notices how much I've improved.

"Not just yet," I wave off her prompt with a grateful grin. "I just want to go back to daydreaming again."

"Whatcha thinking about?" She lands and takes a seat next to me.

"What it will be life once I get myself some friends," I beam, admiring the drawing on the cave's walls. It's mainly stick figures, and a majority of them are sad. "Did I make thoses?"

Numuin joins me in the brightness of our beams that seem to lighten up the cave better than the sun outside. "Yes, yes you did."

I chuckle joyfully, "I'm a terrible artist."

"Yeah well, I'm sure that some people would admire your creativity," Numuin takes flight once again. "Now, let's get a move on."

I chuckle once again as I get to my feet, "Alright, alright." We make our way to exit the cave somehow feeling more joyful than before. I take one last look at the drawings, they're all smiling now, even the little suns are happy.

"You're growing quite quickly," Numuin mentions as we continue to walk. It's mainly been in silence. I've just been enjoying the sounds of the animals and flowing water, this truly is an amazing place.

"Isn't that a good thing?" I give her a glance as we continue to walk.

"It's an amazing thing actually," She squeaks and dances. "Now you just need to have a little bit of patience."

I've already figured out what she means by that. If we keep walking then I will eventually find my way out. Now I just need to stay positive in order to keep it that way. Though, with how I'm feeling right now, nothing could ruin my mood. I hear a bunch of birds chirping and when I look over, I see a nest with two finches perched in front of a bunch of their babies. What a glorious site. I'm looking forward to having a family like that, even if I'm the one that has to make it. I will achieve that future, I know I will.

After about ten minutes of walking, we begin to see a clearing. My heart starts to race and I feel like dancing with joy. Hell, what's stopping me from doing so?

Numuin joins me in the dancing as we skip and move through the clearing. Flowers are set to air and gloriously float back to Earth. As we move closer a bed in the center of a portal appears on the ground. It looks familiar but I'm still not quite sure from where. I'm sure that I'll know eventually though.

We both stop just in front of the portal, and I turn to face Numuin. "Thank you," I speak with wholeheartedness. "I truly am grateful. I hope that you have an amazing life with the rest of the fairies."

"I will alway be here to guide you back if you were to ever get lost again," she reaches out her hand to shake mine, I give her my pinky finger and we both giggle.

"I'll miss you," I give her one last smile and wipe away my tears.

She just gives me a bright smile and I turn back to the portal. Before I get onto it, I'm prompted by some sparkly words to shout my name. Without thinking I shout, "Alex!" But nothing happens. Then, something pops into my head, and before I try to understand what it is, I decide to just let it out. "Alex Croissance!" The words decide to the ground and I move towards the portal.

As I step onto it, it feels like carpet. I make my way to the bed and crawl into it, feeling as though I'm growing smaller with every step. I lay my head on the soft and comforting pillow and throw the warm covers over top of me. Slowly drifting off to sleep, the last thing I see is Numuin smiling proudly at me.

I awaken in a small room with the sun just peeking up over the horizon. Everything is small and I'm surrounded by my toys. A soft, little teddy bear is cradled in my arms and the sound of laughter and music floods my ears. I slide off of my bed and waddle over to my door, reaching towards the handle to open it. As I open it and slowly make my way down the hall, the noise gets louder and my mood is getting even more joyful and energized.

I peek past a corner and see my parents dancing in the living room, they immediately notice me. Their smiles only grow wider as my mother comes to pick me up and dance with me in her arms. The soothing movements and sounds cradle me off to sleep and my teddy rests in my arms as I rest in my parents' arms.

Particles

Yellow tape branches off into the darkness; Signs marked with, 'Beware,' 'Turn Around,' and 'Danger,' riddle the overgrown land of sharp grass and bushy trees. It wasn't long ago that my mother and I were walking through this area with the dogs, admiring the well-kept greenery and laughing as the children of the town would chase butterflies or get preoccupied with birds.

It was less than a week ago when everything changed.

"Oi!" The deep voice of one of my groupmates echoes through the mucky wind.

"Marco, shut up!" My other groupmate smacks him. The sound makes me wince.

I turn around to find them both standing just next to the tape, staring at me expectantly but also a bit uneasily. Ginea's short, spiky red hair sticks out like my flames in a cave, her glasses sitting perfectly on the bridge of her nose and her school uniform tailored perfectly to her slim, studious figure. Marco, standing just beside her, is wearing the same uniform—a black cloak, a black mask to hide our identities, filter the air, and keep our DNA to ourselves, a black bulletproof vest, black cargo pants, black combat boots, and possibly most important of all, our black belts made to hold supplies such as weapons and potions—his spiky, short silver hair also sticks out, but more like a dove hiding among the owls. His skin is mahogany and slightly transparent due to his invisibility. His eyes, his damn eyes, are completely white. Revealing nothing into his soul.

"Hurry the hell up already," Ginea speaks with a hush as she leads the way past the police tape, keeping an eye on all of our surroundings as her glasses glimmer under the high half moon.

There's gravel below us, cracking and knocking with each careful step we take. I stay in the rear, squinting my eyes as the dark, destroyed town materializes around us. Our primary weapons are on our backs; a staff for me. It was a hand-me-down and one that I'd rather just use as a marshmallow roasting stick and get rid of from my life for good. A DSR-1 for Marco, a weapon that doesn't necessarily suit his rowdy personality. And a compound bow for Ginea, her enchanted arrows shining with a faint variety of colours.

"Let's check out that building first," Ginea points to an old, western-looking county jail and we follow her lead. "It should at least give us some early reports into all of the shit that was caused here."

"If it all wasn't already destroyed," I mention softly, glancing into the shadows and alleys of buildings. I feel as though there are eyes everywhere, as small as the particles of the air, watching me.

I hear a groan let out from Marco and a sigh from Ginea, "Let's try to stay positive here, okay, Timber? Don't forget, if there's nothing here then we'll most likely fail."

"Yeah, Timber, quit being a downer and let the actual smart kids do all of the work," Marco snarkily chimes in.

Says the dude that makes Ginea do all of his work for him and in return shows her basic human decency.

We step into the dark, destroyed, and rampaged mess of a jail. Prison bars are covered in blood, some appear to be cleanly bitten off. But that's impossible. No one here possessed any form of magic.

Ginea circles around one of the large, scratched-up desks, similar to the claws of a werewolf, and begins picking at the lock. To no avail. "Timber, I need your help."

I go to help and suddenly my face begins to scrunch up and my airways tighten. My face angles up to the ceiling and I shut my eyes as I let out a hollering, echoing sneeze, simultaneously releasing sparks and lighting up the dusty floorboards below us.

"Timber!" Ginea shouts, rushing over to stomp out the fire and wincing. Marco stands in the corner, eyes wide and mouth gaping with awe. "What the hell?"

"I-I-I-" Once more, another wrenching sneeze releases and Ginea jumps out of the way. "I don't know what's happening."

"Get out!" Ginea cries, ushering Marco and I out of the jail as the flames spread.

We run out of the building, the ember within me burning brighter as I attempt to hold in my recurring sneezes. "It-it-it must be the air."

Ginea anxiously shakes her head, "Impossible."

"Oi, Timber, don't go cooking us well done, alright?" Marco laughs arrogantly.

I can't hold it any longer.

The sound rings in my ears, my eyes remaining shut as the terrified screams release from my groupmates. The force is so hard that I drop to my knees, soon noticing a bright red on my shut eyelids. Slowly, I open them and notice little bits of white glimmer in the air, being illuminated by my fire-clothed body. Slowly, I stand up, gazing around. The entire town is engulfed in a white powder of sorts; millions of white particles. Luckily the flames fit through my mask. I wouldn't like to think what would have happened if I had breathed in whatever those chemicals may be.

Marco is still dumbfounded, idiot. But Ginea is looking around at all of the specks as well. "We need to get out of here and speak to Mr. MacIntosh and Ms. Xic. Let's walk to the gates and I'll fly us back."

"Yeah," We all agree and I lead the way. Freaked out as the sense of being watched grows more powerful.

By the time we've reached the gates, something feels off. I spin around and it's just Marco, staring me up and down with a raised eyebrow. "Don't you go roasting me, Flamestress."

"Where's Ginea?"

He turns around and shrugs, "must've found a library."

I march past him and he leaps out of the way, I run, faster, over exhilarating myself and allowing the flames to die down. There are faint marks in the dry, dead-plant dirt, not regular steps like if she were to just turn around and walk away, but long drags with the imprint below our boots being lengthened. Wherever she went, she was dragged there, and judging by the constant straight pattern, she was knocked unconscious as well.

Passing by all of the buildings within the small, western town, with a growing flame reaching out of the jail, I eventually find the tracks leading up to a cathedral. The holiness of its past has certainly dissipated long ago. The Christ that was once atop its large, oak doors has been rusted and appears as though it has bleeding eyes and a slit throat. Hanging upside down, still leaking some sort of dark liquid.

The doors of the cathedral are parted slightly and I glance over my shoulder to see Marco tiredly running to catch up to me. He stops just next to me and waves a few particles out of his face. Grunting as they then latch onto his clothing.

"What the hell has gotten into you?" He murmurs timidly and flinches at his own deep, echoing voice. "That's not a library, are you blind now? Did you breathe in some of the particles?"

"Just shut up, turn invisible, and pull out your weapon," I order, removing my staff from my back and carefully pushing open the doors, wincing as it creates an eerie creak.

After a moment of hesitation, he follows my orders, stepping silently behind me, his presence known to me but visually nonexistent. As my eyes are adjusting to the change in lighting, a putrid, rotten smell leeches into my nostrils and I gag. I grip the staff tightly in my hands, feeling the smooth, impenetrable wood against my skin. There's a slight dripping coming from the other end of the room.

Drip. Drip. Drip.

It's not long before Marco lets out a gasp that makes me jump. My eyes, finally adjusted, make me question reality. There's Ginea, completely naked and hanging from the moulded ceiling, her body is gray as if she's been completely drained of blood. There's a chain with spikes tied around her neck, her skin torn back like a cut on a foam ball. My eyes then lower, where I see the townspeople, the mountain of townspeople below her. Almost as though they were zombies, climbing on top of one another for the last brain on Earth—their bodies hollow and devoid of life. Marco makes himself visible and points back up to Ginea, which makes me notice even more than the first time. All of her organs have been removed. There's a gaping hole in her gut and even her head appears to be sowed on haphazardly. Her eyes are closed, but judging by the bit of blood on her face, they too were taken from her.

"Ginea," Her name comes out like a final breath of air. My own body feels hollow, yet heavy and difficult to hold up.

"Timber, come on, we have to get out of here," Marco grabs me, forcing my body to immediately light up and he begins to scream.

My mask begins to slip somehow, possibly due to all of the movement, and I watch as the little white particles whirl their way into my mouth. Contaminating my lungs.

I let out one last order, "Marco, run!"

And everything goes black.

Down With Them Youngins

The sun rolls above us like a cyclone, radiating its heat down to this desolate desert. K.A.R.F has managed to overheat 6 times within the two hours since sunrise and even with its fifteen separate cooling systems its metal manages to compete with that of the ball of rage above us.

It has been 12 years since the sun has begun dismantling itself and each day I grow more irritated by tourists that only speak of its beauty.

But this story isn't about the sun, or the annoying tourists, or the deathly heat, or the fact that the world has practically ended yet we somehow still remain. This story is about the people within the small town of Jashk that refuse to even give us a drop of water or even coolant. Those red-skinned freaks.

"Gip. Breathe." K.A.R.F. struggles to get out the words even after disabling his A.I. voice software. "Look. At. Your. Surroundings."

"Easier said than done," I mumble in return. All around us, there is only scorching hot sand, the orange sky, and the sun, halfway finished with its four-hour day. My ass burns while sitting down, even worse with a stupid smoking machine beside me. So much for being vast and revolutionary.

"Shall. We. Continue?"

"Not like we have anything else to do." I lift myself back up with a grunt, taking in the scars running all up and down my arms. What used to be a bullet hole in the palm of my hand, now filled with metal and sand.

The wind blows and a tear escapes my eye. It burns so fucking much.

"Would. You. Like. Me. To. Turn. On. GPS. Now?"

I let out a groan and begin marching through the waterless beach, "No."

"Turning. On. GPS. Now."

"Wait, no!" Spinning without stable footing, I leap before I fall, landing straight against one of K.A.R.F.'s exterior buttons. "Cancel! Cancel!"

"Voice. Recognition. Error."

"Don't turn on the GPS you stupid fucking piece of junk!" Going to slam a kick into its large body, I slip mid-thrust, dropping to the ground, and only tapping it. "Reboot! Reboot!"

"GPS. Signals. Booting. Up." A rod shoots up from the top of the large, rectangular, metallic rectangle, beaming red in circles like a lighthouse. "Location. Set."

"Shit." My eyes go wide and heart begins to race. Without a thought, I turn around and begin booking it downhill, instantly stumbling. Falling. And rolling. Sand gets into my eyes and cuts, my limbs are launched into my body and bones are crushed. And the drop feels as though it is taking forever.

Until I hit my head and am engulfed by darkness.

"Vitals. Are. Stabilizing." I awaken to the sound and sight of K.A.R.F. towering over me, covering me in darkness. "He. Has. Awoken. However. Vitamins. Are. Low."

"Aren't everyone's vitamins low these days?" A deeply, feminine voice chuckles not too far from me. "What else are you able to track, big guy?"

"I. Am. An. A.I. Powered. Machine. You. Teach. I. Learn."

The woman then speaks as though she is intrigued, "Have you ever learned how to gut a human?"

My eyes shoot open and my body soon follows, "Alright, that's enough."

"Aw, come on," The voice suddenly switches to behind me. "We're just having a little fun."

"Yes. I. Have."

"Hold up!" The woman spawns in front of me with her back facing me, her dark hands placed on her wide hips as she stares up at K.A.R.F. "How the hell have you managed to teach this huge chunk of metal how to gut a human?"

I let out a sigh, waiting for the blurriness of my vision to subside. "I can't show you without him following through, it's a bug that I can't fix without the needed parts and chemicals."

She turns to face me and my eyes immediately lock on her dark, huge, cut nose, "Whatcha need?"

"Oh, no, no, no, no you don't," Attempting to rise, I soon drop back down onto whatever hard surface I've been laid on, unable to stand. "Ah fuck." Deep breath. "I refuse to get locked in a chamber again because of some sort of 'hidden deal.'"

The woman snorts and lifts up a candle placed below her, just out of sight. Ah, that's why I couldn't see, it was just dark. Her dark green tank top and cut-up black shorts don't reveal enough skin within this heat, I wonder how often she gets heat stroke dressed like that. Her shoes are even worse, sandals? Sure, they're good for beaches and such, but definitely not this level of a 'beach.'

She catches me staring and raises an eyebrow, "Don't you think you're a little busy just trying to survive to gawk at me?"

Blinking, I shake my head. "Gawk? I wasn't gawking at you. I was just concerned for your safety, but clearly, it doesn't matter what anyone thinks."

She rolls her eyes, "Men."

I stop for a moment to scan my surroundings, it's shockingly cool in here, still humid, but much better than outside. We appear to be inside of some sort of garage, one that used to have those machines that would raise cars so then mechanics or bots can work on them and then charge five times higher than what it'd normally cost. Much more slowly this time, I rise up from the platform I had been placed on, a desk covered in oil that appears to have had all of its contents hastily pushed to the side. My eyes survey the walls, old, rusted, and slightly misshapen due to melting by the heat. It's dark in here, but just light enough for me to be able to see the wires and switches on K.A.R.F. as well as the woman examining him.

"So who are you? Where are we?" I ask slowly, searching for a weapon of some sort.

She turns her head and smirks. "Oh just someone in the area, no need to worry about me," facing me, she takes a few steps forwards, making an echo bounce off the walls. "But what I'm more curious about is who are you? Also, what is that thing?" Her thumb is directed straight to K.A.R.F who is set still in a corner.

"My. Name. Is. K.A.R.F."

"Silence," I cut him off.

"No, no, no, I have a right to know," She crosses her arms and turns back to face the vast hunk of metal. "What are you and who is he?" After a few moments of no response, she tries something else. "Volume up and lock audio settings."

My eyes go wide and a breeze flows past me. I can do that?

"My. Name. Is. K.A.R.F. Meaning. Of. Name. Unknown. I-"

"Stop, stop, stop, fuck that's so annoying," She cuts him off and turns to face me, my lungs cease for a moment, "do you have any way to fix that or are you just an idiot when it comes to machinery?"

"I. Assure. You. He. Is. Not-"

Clenching my teeth and furrowing my eyebrows, I mutter, "K.A.R.F. Shut the fuck up."

The woman disappears suddenly and I then feel a breath on the back of my neck, making me reel forward. "So who are you then?" Something pinches my neck, a blade, nothing else it can be. Without any mode of control, my arms shoot up, grab onto the woman's forearm with one hand, and pushes down on a pressure point and frees the knife with the other.

Then, in one full motion, I throw the woman over my shoulder, slamming her straight onto the desk while also knocking over and shattering a lamp.

It's like a tornado of noise for the next ten seconds straight, followed by a moment of silence, and one final crash off in the other end of the garage. Leaning over the desk, I lock eyes with a fierce glare and a woman covered in glass attached to it.

It had been years since I had to make a move like that, even longer since I had first been taught it.

"System. Temperatures. Stabilized." K.A.R.F's robotic voice screeches out, most likely due to it adjusting to all of the commotion. "Activating. A.I. Voice. Adjustment. Software. Now."

The woman groans and slowly begins to sit up, "I will get answers out of that damn giant piece of junk, even if I have to threaten it with a bucket of water."

"No!"

"Good evening," We all pause as the voice of my mother begins to rise from K.A.R.F's speakers. Soft and sweet, it makes my eyes burn.

Oh, Mother, I'm so sorry.

"My name is K.A.R.F, but you can call me Karf, and that is my creator Gip. He is a war veteran, a general of the marine corps to be precise, and has fought in more wars than seconds that humans have lived in the universe." I seriously want to be the one to dump a bucket of water on him now. It's one thing to go against my orders and reveal ourselves, but to do it with my late mother's voice? "We are in search of water and coolant, respectively and have been searching for a place to stay and things to do with our time with what time remains."

"Wait a second," The woman's eyes squint as she gets up and begins searching through a pile of papers, eventually finding one stained with salt water and burnt edges. She scans it with her eyes, occasionally shooting glances up at myself and K.A.R.F., but I already know what it is that she's looking at. "The last veteran ever alive and the- damn it, it's smudged. Whatever, wanted for their hearts. Reward: Water and AC."

I let out a quiet exhale and begin to slowly shake my head. I'm too damn old for this shit.

My ears twitch as the paper is soon torn, "Oh well, I have enough of that anyway."

I shoot a quick glance at K.A.R.F and return the same wide-eyed expression back to the woman, "Huh?"

"Well, yeah," The woman claps her hands and instantly the entire garage lights up. Revealing not only jugs or coolers of water but entire hearths that begin to heat up. "I doubt they'd give anything to someone like me anyway."

I'm dumbfounded. Eyes blinking and mouth opened in silence.

The woman laughs, her deep voice almost villainous like that of a cartoon. Cartoons, I miss those. Then, her face goes hard as stone and serious. "But don't think I have forgiven you for the ruckus you've caused." She begins walking towards a set of metal stairs, "I've searched far and wide to find that damn GPS signal, and honestly, I don't think we like you."

"Wait, but you said-"

"That I was in the area?" Her face turns towards mine, then she closes her eyes and marches up the creaking steps. "Surely someone as… aged… as you would know better."

"We?"

I drop my head to the ground, starting as a way to question things internally but soon am scanning through all of the words and papers covered in glass. Wanted. Wanted. Job Request. Metal Order. Job Request. Wanted. Death Threats. Seems she's quite a busy woman, or perhaps they're quite busy people.

Almost like clockwork, six people step out from the shadow where they had previously been hiding behind the hearths. They're all wearing black hoods but judging by their builds, I'd say three women, one girl, one boy, and one man.

She picks up one of the rods that had been previously resting in a large, fiery hearth, it's completely red, almost white and is shaped like an arrow. I instantly search through the ground again, finding a few papers stamped with an arrow in the centre of a circle and the tip aflame. The major one that sticks out to me is a wanted poster and as covertly as I possibly can, I nudge it loose with my foot. There's no picture of the people, just the emblem with the words, "Wanted: Dead, Reward: 780,000 kins, 60 gallons of water, 3-night stay at last remaining five-star resort."

I couldn't care less about the money, but the water and a place to rest would certainly be nice. My eyes rise back up to the woman as she smiles confidently with her flaming rod. And she had just brought me right to them.

"It appears that tension in the room has hit an all-time high, releasing calming mist in five seconds," K.A.R.F speaks over the silence, audio now regulated.

"Cancel!" The woman shouts.

"What is your name?" I yell in return.

"Cancelling peace protocol one."

"Why does that matter?"

"Well, you know my name and K.A.R.F's."

"So? Not my fault you're stupid and choose to carry a target by your side."

"Not my fault either that you had brought an ex-vet, someone trained in combat and capturing enemies, straight to your base." Her nose twitches. "Now what is your name? I don't care about them, I just want to know yours."

"J."

"Just 'J?'"

She exhales, "Jig."

"Good enough," I smirk, stepping over the papers and shards of glass and begin making my way over to K.A.R.F.

Teleporting in front of me, she yells, "Where the fuck do you think you're going?"

"How about you tell me how you do that first."

"Never," she crosses her arms, sticking out her chin. Rookie mistake.

Blade to her throat in an instant, "I mean if you say so, but you were just so kind to let me have this that you might as well continue with the generosity."

"I'm no idiot."

"No? Then how did you forget about your knife so quickly?"

"Because it isn't hers," K.A.R.F mentions. "It's her sisters, I've watched the entire exchange with my offline surveillance after we both went under."

"Wait," I look towards K.A.R.F. "Why were you under?"

My head slams against the ground and spine aches. Fuck, I'm such an idiot.

"We powered him down shortly after locating the both of you, not like it mattered, he'd already overheated."

"Again?" I groan towards K.A.R.F.

"Listen!" Jig grabs me by the collar of my shirt, giving me instant sight of her breasts. "I've had enough of this, either hear me out or die." She directs the blade to my eye as her teeth clench with fury.

"I don't think I was told that was the goal," I squint, raising an eyebrow.

She scoffs, shoving me back into the ground. "I need your help, since well, you're an old man and all."

Confused, I blink. "Isn't that a man right there?" I question, pointing towards the tall, muscular, hooded figure in a corner upstairs.

Her eyes flutter for a moment as though she's questioning something but then shakes her head, "He's too young, we need someone older, like you."

"Gee, thanks."

"Only offence."

"What is it that you need me to do?"

She sucks in her lips, releasing silence all around us with the only noise being that of the beeping of K.A.R.F. It's so annoying, I really wish I had that coolant.

"We need food."

"Food? That's all? That's what you did all of-"

"Just hear me out," after I don't say anything, she continues. "With the new laws in all of the areas around us, we're not allowed more than one vegetable a week per person, but elderly people, especially veterans, are allowed an entire meal three times a week."

"So you want me to start providing food for you all?" I begin to get up and head toward my machine.

"It's not that easy," She stops me, placing her rough hand on my shoulder. "Since we had brought you here after that GPS went off, everyone knows that we have something to do with each other and even if we both claim to not know each other, they won't provide you with even a single leaf."

"So just act as though we had attacked each other and go and bash your guys' image in order to make it seem as though we're not 'working together,'" I raise an eyebrow and flick her hand off of me.

She stutters, "Well, I- uh- yeah, exactly."

I shrug, "Alright."

"Wait!" She stops me again and my eye twitches due to the physical contact. "That's all? You don't want anything in return? What do you think this sort of deal is?"

"Well, I assumed it's just I go into town, make people believe we have nothing to do with each other, bring you guys some food to last you all for a bit while you provide me with shelter during the nights, then head out on my merry way." And then I'll come back to kill you all in order to reap the rewards from that sweet, sweet bounty. No more sleeping in the sand, relying on a smoking machine for shade.

"Well, I guess that fits well for us, for now at least."

I march away from her, stopping in front of K.A.R.F. and placing my hands on my hips, "So which town shall I go into first?"

It's not too big, reminds me of old western cowboy towns found in those history or renaissance museums. A few buildings on each side with a taller building in the center, most of the time is like a type of church, though at this point I doubt anyone has held onto their religions. If anything it's probably now used for sacrificing people who have taken more than they were allowed to. It's pretty quiet at the moment, people are probably remaining indoors and doing whatever they can to stay cool.

The best next course of action would be the saloon two buildings down from me. The ground crunches below me and everything around here is either brown or red, nothing else. There was a burned wooden sign a few feet before entering the town that had read, 'Burnshine,' with a bullet hole to dot the 'i.' If I knew the area better then this place is definitely not the town I'd go to first, if anything those people might be trying to get me killed. But seeing the way they all behaved, the fear they had presented along with the false confidence that Jig had shown, I believe that they really do just want some food.

I stop in front of the saloon which is just a sad-looking cube. The windows are completely blocked out to avoid any rays of light and the few openings there are have been made by bullets. The steps crack under my weight which I'm confident isn't my fault, and I push through the doors. Other than the bit of chatter off by the bar that had now gone still, it appears that nobody wishes to speak. However, even with all eyes on me, there's still a young man running around, cleaning up, and serving drinks to the guests. He's fit—skinny—but fit considering this day and age. It's certainly impressive, I'd trust that young man with a gun in a war, after getting rid of any fear in his mind of course.

Choosing to ignore the burning stares, I make my way to the edge of the bar, just two seats down from 3-elderly men, one with long silver hair, one with short white hair, and one completely bald, all utterly skinny. The bartender seems to be the oldest one here though, possibly reaching 110 years. Mainly men in this bar, not surprising. The only women appear to be a young woman that must be spending time with her father at a table off to the side, and an older woman smoking by a crack in a blocked-out window. The place has a pool table that seems to be more of an art piece to represent the formation of dust.

There are lights in here, LEDs to minimise the creation of heat. They're placed along the tops of walls and around the bottoms of tables. A creative way indeed to make sure everyone can still see.

The bartender croaks finally after a few silent minutes with the only sound being that of the running-around busboy. "What brings you-"

"This," I interrupt him, sliding across the bar the wanted poster I've found of that forge group. The man raises his eyebrow and skims it while wiping down a glass. "How recent is it?"

He exhales through his nose, staring down at the opaque, improperly cleaned piece, "What information do you have so far?"

"All I want to know is how recent is it and are the rewards still available," I squint at him, watching as his forearms tense and release as he continues to polish horribly. "Or had whoever is searching for them already croaked and burned up in this lovely weather?"

The area is completely silent once more, even the young man had finally halted, resulting in a glare from the barkeep. Then, the three men near me break into deep, dry-throated laughter. The bartender shakes his head and sets the glass down in front of me. Turning his back as he searches for something to pour despite the majority of the bottles being just for show.

"I tell yee what, dat poster is as outdated as mah motters himey," The bald man guffaws, slamming his fist on the counter and spilling a bit of whatever dark liquid he is drinking. The young man bolts over and pulls out a cloth from his side to begin cleaning when the bald man slings his arm around his shoulders and pulls him down to eye level. "Dis yong marn is perbably yunger dan dat der paper."

I blink for a moment, waiting for my dehydrated brain to process whatever I had just heard into English, hm, this may be good. Raising an eyebrow and frowning, I deepen my voice, "What do you think of someone like me, young man?"

"Um, I, uh," He stutters, pulling through the baldies grip. "I'm sure you're very wise, tough, and know your way around life."

"You just said wise twice there, boy," I grimace, turning to the bartender. "These young people nowadays wouldn't know how to move their damn legs if it weren't for people like us always having to repeat our damn selves."

"You got that right," The bartender points to me with a cocky smile then nods over to his employee. Perfect, they're acting exactly as I thought they would. "This young man wouldn't know hard work even if the center of the Earth were to assign him a job."

"But I've been working here just as long as you," He mumbles, dropping his head down slightly. "I work twice as many hours as you too."

"Now shut dat der moth of yurs, yung mern!" The bald man interjects, pushing the boy away from him who ends up slamming into the wall. "Yee nev see whert we wise folk do! We've busd oor arses fur years and stil du tu dis tay. If yee'd ope yer eeys den yee'd kno jurst how herd we work."

That man probably had far more than enough to drink.

The boy clenches his fists as a vein pops out on his neck, he then glares straight at the bald man and shouts, "Well maybe if you'd put down that damn glass of poison then you'd realise that your wife had left you for a reason and she wasn't the damn problem! And hell, maybe if you'd actually look around you like the damn 'wise' man you are then you'd realise that while you all are busy drinking and grumbling your days away us 'immature folk' are busy trying to work our asses off to not only earn the respect of you assholes but also try and make the Earth livable once again! But you all keep on adding in laws that prevent us from doing so because 'combining new and old technology is a waste of resources.' So how about you all get off your fucking asses and focus on yourselves for a change instead of tearing down the younger generations!"

The young man finally finishes and begins to take a few deep breaths. It seems that he's been holding all of that in for a while now. Perfect.

"Another one of his temper tantrums," The bartender shakes his head and leans on the edge of the bar closest to me. "You're like a damn toddler."

The boy tosses his arms up into the air then proceeds to rip off his apron and storm off, exclaiming, "I fucking quit, just watch this place turn into a shitter after I'm gone."

"And der he goes," The bald man lets out a sigh. "Deese youngins owlways quit der momernt terms git herd."

"So disrespectful," I shake my head. Now's my moment. "All these kids nowadays."

"Meh, he'll be back eventually, begging to be forgiven with his tail between his legs," The bartender sighs and goes to finish wiping up the spilled droplets of a drink. "These kids will never get anywhere in life being that damn sensitive."

"Moost senstive gerneration yeet," The bald man adds, clenching his fists with a fiery look in his eyes. "I swear, eel fuckin' kill em fer what he sad."

Ironic.

"Honestly, I don't think young people should be allowed to own anything, like that group that owns the forgery for instance," I watch as the bartender wrings out the spilled droplets into a dark bottle—good thing I didn't drink anything. But hey, you gotta do what you gotta do, and the FDA went bankrupt long, long ago due to approving birth control for men which of course led to the elderly of that time snapping and completely destroying them.

"Honestly, I couldn't agree with you more." The bartender smiles, setting the bottle back on the shelf and tossing his rag on the counter. The empty glass is still in front of me for some reason.

"I say we should take down any businesses run by those children much like what those wise people back then had done with the FDA and similar businesses," I fold my hands in front of me. Here we go, just one simple agreement.

"Oh yeah, or like the government, just completely abolish them and kill anyone who dares to start it up again."

Hook, line, and sinker.

"Erm in," The bald man chimes in and the other two nod in agreement.

"Fantastic!" I smile widely. "But also, another quick question."

"What is it?"

"Where can I find a place that provides food?"

"And the end, so what do you think?"

"I think you should probably work on the plot holes."

"But, K.A.R.F. wasn't it at least a decent story?"

"Well, Gip, you've never been one for storytelling. You're more of a shoot, shoot, type of person."

"Yeah, whatever, increase AC to level seven."

"Increasing AC level now."

Scarlet, Azure

"Finally, I'm back," I let out a gasp for air as my feet touch down on the ground and switch out of my eagle form, tossing a heavy bag onto my bed. "I swear, the oxygen all the way up there is practically deadly."

"Huh? What? Huh?" Henry screams, clutching at his head as he looks all around him. Hastily, I transform into a puppy, scurry over, and begin rubbing on his leg. It doesn't take long for him to pause for a moment, take a few deep breaths, then pick me up, placing me on his lap, and scratching my ears. "I'm so sorry, it's just that, they came by again today."

Hopping off of him, I transform back into my human form and take a seat next to him on his bed, making sure to not touch him and instead just sit silently with him. Our beds are on opposite sides of this concrete building, the only window being blocked by metal bars, spaced out enough so only I can get in and out. The only light there is comes in through the small, unbreakable window in our steel door. Our beds, depressing as they are, are quite possibly the most comfortable things in this entire facility. Granted, they're just rusted metal frames and a thin mattress with no covers, but that doesn't change that it's better than sleeping on the ground.

Henry mumbles, his heart rate finally low enough for him to not scream, "They strapped me to the chair again."

I clench my fists. The chair. That fucking chair.

"They wouldn't stop screaming at me, calling me a disappointment and that I should be like you. That I might as well die."

It's not fair at all. I'm not like this because of them.

"Maybe I should."

Breathing out through my nose, I rise up from his bed and march over to my own, moving around the bag I had previously tossed and pulling things out with my back blocking his view to make sure he doesn't see.

"Like, I've been here longer than you and yet nothing has changed for me."

A lot has certainly changed for me though, especially since you're by my side.

Then, the squeaking of the mattress and frame, followed by a few weak, wary footsteps.

"I think I should just hit the Scarlet Button next time."

There it is.

Grabbing onto a plastic container I spin around and push it into his chest, doing my best to force an uplifting smile, but I've never been the best with emotions. Outside of fictional stories of course.

"Here, I got your favourite," He gives me a look of shock and his eyes sparkle for a moment as though he's about to cry. I reach behind me with my freehand to grab a pair of chopsticks, placing them on top of his pack of sushi.

Slowly, he raises his hands up and grabs onto the variety pack of sushi, then moves his head to the side to gaze behind me, "Did you not grab yourself anything?"

"No I did," I nod, doing my best to smile but it probably looks horrifying.

He smiles slightly and raises an eyebrow, "Other than books."

Turning my head to look behind me, I exclaim, "Oh well would you look at that, it appears to be only books. Oh where, oh where has the food gone." We look back at each other again and I shrug. "Oh well."

"76?"

"Go eat your sushi, you deserve it," I wave him off and take a seat on my bed, fishing through my newest weekly book haul. I don't have the heart to tell him why.

Why I don't—no—can't eat anymore.

And I have no intention of ever telling him.

That chair. They've been taking me to it every night now.

All because I'm getting 'weak.'

He doesn't even know that my name is now supposed to be 42.

It doesn't feel right keeping this sort of information from him, but I have no other choice. The truth would quite literally kill him.

And he still has so much more to live for.

If he'd just do something he used to love.

If he'd then just press the Azure Button.

"Hey, 76, there's something I've been meaning-" He pauses for a moment, choking back tears as he cries into his tray of sushi. "Meaning to ask you for a while now."

Emotions. They're so strange. "What is it?"

"Why don't you try to help us break free with your shapeshifting?"

I've tried. So many times.

"Because they've covered all of the bases, people can't see me out in public because of a chip in my skin, which is why I can only use self-checkout or steal, and I can't use it to fight the facility itself because there are so many limitations to my powers."

I have, however, been doing little things here and there to try and contact the outer world. Leaving notes in unpopular books with vague messages that are supposed to connect, but I can only do that twice a year without getting caught. Hell, I've even tried putting down fingerprints and such all around areas that I'd destroy, but after just five minutes it would all be repaired, with the memories of anyone who may have seen my destruction being cleared.

"I really wish we could figure out a way out of here," he mumbles, chomping down on another piece of sushi. He appears to be eating much slower today, energy must be zapped due to the chair. That fucking chair. "If only people would just discover what's going on and try to do something about it."

If only. But unfortunately, if people do figure out, then we'll all be killed in an instant to cover their tracks.

"Hey, 76, can you please promise me something?"

"What is it?" I look up at him, folding my hands overtop of my stack of books in front of me.

"Promise me that we'll always stick by each other's side, no matter how gruesome things get."

If only it were that easy.

Forcing another horrific smile, I reply calmly, "I promise."

Give Everything, End Up With Nothing

A door off in the distance slams open and in comes marching L, as pissed off as can be. He glares at G as he proceeds to look through and grant peoples' prayers, smiling with a few soft tears in his eyes.

L stomps over, slamming down a piece of paper on their conjoined desk. "What the fuck is this?" L shouts with his deep voice, instantly snapping G back to reality.

With a wave of G's hands, all of the gold and white hovering papers around him disappear and he steps over to L, gazing down to the sheet of blue paper. "New Invention. Technology to make all your dreams come true. Blah, blah, blah. Just believe in science and logic." G's face scrunches and he looks up at L with a confused expression, "What the-"

"How have you not known about this already and stopped it?" L yells, picking up the paper and shoving it in G's chest, then takes a seat at his desk, making an eerie screech ring throughout the building. "I swear to god-"

"Eh."

"Now is a perfectly good time to say that!" L practically screams into his palms as he covers up his face.

Holding the paper out in front of him and flattening it out again G rereads and rereads again, then, with a sigh, he moves over to his desk and takes a seat. Placing the paper out flat in front of him with a deep expression of contemplation.

"We really have fallen huh?" G mumbles, flattening his hands out in front of him and begins gazing all around at his depressing surroundings. A dark warehouse, that is where they are now forced to reside after G had chosen to grant too many prayers. The only lights they have are the ones on their chipped wooden desks that face each other. That's all they have left, one warehouse, two desks, two lamps, two chairs and they both know that G would even give up those in an instant if someone really needed it.

"Yeah, and I wonder who caused this to happen," L slams his fists on his desk, making the entire set up shake. "If you hadn't tried to take over every department then this wouldn't have happened. Not everyone should have their wish granted!"

"Prayer."

"It's a wish. They've gotten greedy and entitled because you've kept giving shit-"

"Language."

"To them," L rolls his eyes. "Almost nothing these people ask for nowadays are actually things these people need, hell-"

"Eh."

Another eyeroll, "I bet every single person out there is just slowly making their way to that laboratory because what they have is just never enough."

"But I want all my subjects to live their best lives possible," G holds up the paper, staring at it with deep contemplation.

L exhales a groan, "They would if they weren't constantly trying to get their hands on material items or praying for things that require just a little dedication and hardwork."

"Well, what do you think we should do about this then?" G flips the paper to face L and he takes it.

He shrugs, "Blow them up."

"No."

"Hm, we could-" he cuts himself off, shaking his head. "No, that'll never work."

"Well, what is it?"

"We could challenge them."

"How so?"

"Well, there are a few different ways we can go about this," He starts, raising his eyebrows at the words upon the flyer. "Help the population see that it's actually more rewarding to earn something instead of just having it handed to them. Or-"

"That sounds pretty difficult to do though, like you said it yourself, they've gotten greedy," G places his head on his hands and once again examines his surroundings.

"Glad you can finally admit it to yourself," L smiles but immediately stops himself before G notices and goes back to his serious expression. "Or we could attempt to halt their operations long enough for people to believe that they're just a bunch of scammers, which they could be, but seeing technology these days, it's entirely likely that it's legitimate."

"But I doubt anyone will ever pray for something like that."

"Hm," L fidgets with the cord of his lamp, focusing in on the hard metallic balls, warm with the radiating light. "I've never used up any of my yearly prayers before."

"But-" G sits up straight, eyes now wide. "That goes against your morals, actually no. It goes against your entire purpose."

"You're right, though I do know something even more likely to happen."

"What's that?"

"Hardcore believers that take forever to adapt," L starts. "It's highly likely that they'll pray for operations to stop, or end altogether. Plus, you and I both know that they may even wish death and suffering upon the people within that laboratory."

G lets out a deep breath, shaking his head, "I've never liked those sorts of prayers, they're even more heartbreaking than the ones of people begging for me to save their loved ones. You know, the ones you demand be ignored."

"You can't save them all, you must sacrifice some in order to save others. You know, like with what you've done to your family."

"That's enough of that."

"You started it."

"Whatever, let's just get started."

"Started on what, oh holy ruler?"

"Stop."

"No."

"Excuse me?"

"I said no." L grimaces, glaring into G's eyes. "We're in this mess because of you, because you've decided to demote me because you don't have the maturity and understanding of how the system works. I had looked out for these people for life times, I've mastered and understand the system better than anyone. I've allowed the overpopulation just to make sure you would stop complaining, which inevitably led to even more problems among the people and all of a sudden we were getting overwhelmed and you just couldn't bear to allow anyone to be unhappy so you just gave them everything till we had nothing. So, no, I won't stop. Because you didn't bother to stop and contemplate your actions and-"

L's eyes go wide, forcing G to question, "What is it?"

Flicking his wrist, a bunch of red and black papers appear around L and after a few silent seconds of reading, he smiles maliciously, "This is perfect."

"Why can you never smile normally?"

"We've received our prayers, and this one in particular is especially dark," He reaches up at one of the pages floating around him and goes to hand it to G.

"No, no, no," G crosses his hands in front of him and pushes the paper back to L. "I always get nightmares when reading prayers that make you smile, just give me the summary.

"G, so not even dear G or anything, they're just the most demanding and in this instance I love it-"

"Yeah, yeah, I get it, go on."

"The people on this Earth has really gone mad, especially with that new stupid, idiotic, satanic laboratory that is attempting to steal souls, blah, blah, blah, starbucks workers, blah, blah, gouging eyes out, blah, blah, blah, gays, blah, blah. Oh, here it is, please burn down the laboratory, and if your holiness is unwilling, then at least please murder all of the 'scientists' that dare to sicken this world."

"I'm not killing anyone."

"Well, they did say at some point to cause a power outage, close to the start actually. Though she did also go pretty in depth on the type of suffering she wants these people to go through and told us exactly what we should do." L adds the page back up to the floating papers around him. "It's basically just a mess all throughout."

G slowly blinks then raises his eyebrows, "I'd rather not know about the second part, but honestly, the first part is exactly what I should do."

Even more mischievously, L grins from ear-to-ear. "Great! I'll call Zeus."

"No!"

Goodbye, My Loved Ones

"Thank you, thank you, a special thanks to every last one of all of my adoring fans!" I shout out among the cheering crowd at the end of another concert. Waving goodbye, I follow my band off stage with our bodyguards close by. All of our fans out there continue to chant our names loud and proud as we make our way to our dressing room.

"Jesus Christ, this tour will be the death of me," The drummer groans, bursting through the red and silver door with our band logo on it and heading straight for the sofa. It appears that they've set out a few water bottles for us along with sandwiches and protein bars.

"Did you all see that brod on the left? I swear she'd climb up on stage if I had simply looked at her," Kyle, the bassist, brags cockily. He then proceeds to pull out another one of his post-show blunts from one of his pockets and retrieves a lighter from the other.

"Are you sure they allow smoking in here? I personally think it'd be better to just do that outside," I frown, still standing by the door as the rest of my band relaxes. Henry, the drummer, covering his face with his hat and his arms crossed as he prepares for a power nap. Jess, my backup singer with gorgeous hair down to her knees, inspects the drinks and snacks they had laid out. She must be starving, especially since she was up before the rest of us to make sure everything was ready and had only eaten a bagel; meanwhile, the rest of us had an entire breakfast waiting for us. Kyle, our bassist, already ignoring my words of warning and instead is lighting his joint without a care in the world. "Do you guys know if weed is even legal here?"

"Chill out, Mr. Star, just come and relax, hell, even just lock the door if you're so scared," Kyle blows out smoke as I look to Jess for backup, only for her to just shrug and continue seeing what kinds of sandwiches there are.

"I just don't feel as though it's ideal to smoke a blunt in this state, what if someone sees?"

"Sounds like," He sits up, pointing the blunt towards me. "That you could use a bit of this, far more than me anyway."

"I don't think you should do that," Jess finally chimes in, immediately putting down a tuna sandwich that had previously caught her eye.

"Aw, is little Jessy going to protect her baby brother now?"

"We're not related," Both her and I groan.

"Yeah whatever, you might as well be with how close the two of you are." He rolls his eyes and gestures at me with the joint once again, "At least try one puff." After I hesitate for another moment, he smirks and then pouts his lips, "Or are you going to let your big sister Jessy continue to baby you?"

"Just do it," Henry yells tiredly, not bothering to move. "As long as it'll shut him up."

Jess turns, placing her hands on her hips, "Henry!"

Raising his head, he stares dead ahead at her, "You know he won't stop till Tyler gives in."

"Well I mean," I mumble, taking a few steps over to Kyle. He's so much happier and more calm than the rest of us after he smokes, perhaps I should-.

"No!" Jess points at me and shouts. "I already don't like it when these idiots smoke around you, so I sure as hell am not going to allow them to drag you into their stupidity."

"Perhaps you could use a puff," Kyle laughs then takes a long, slow drag.

"That's it, I'll just find somewhere else to eat and relax," She stomps towards the door with a face filled with anger. "Come on, Tyler." After she doesn't hear me following her, she spins and glares at all three of us, even Henry who had decided to try at another attempt of napping. She didn't back me up when I was trying to get Kyle to smoke outside, and besides, Henry's right, Kyle won't stop till I give in. Though, maybe this will be good for me, exactly what I need to relax like the rest of them, get the edge off. "Tyler?"

I notice her lips quiver, hoping I'm the only one who saw. Fuck this hurts so much to watch, I hate seeing her upset, especially since we're all here thanks to her. But I know she won't break down, she's too stubborn, but I know she wants to just release really badly.

"I could use a bit of a break from all of the stress," She could too, but I'm not going to suggest that. Fifty shows in one month, it takes a toll on a person, and she's been carrying a majority of the responsibility. Besides, she has far better ways to relax, and we especially can't have our most mature band member going off and burning her brain cells.

She falls silent for a few moments, staring down and refusing to look at me. "I'll text you later to see how you're doing then." And she leaves, shutting the door behind her and proceeds to run down the hall, the noise as clear as day.

"Do you think she's going to snitch?" Henry mumbles, not bothering to look up.

Kyle laughs once more and relights his joint, "Not with Tyler here, now come on, you'll love this new batch I got. It's called 'Kiwi Piss.'"

I let out a cough—struggling to breathe with all of the phlegm in my throat—and go in for another bowl. It's my sixth today and for some reason I still can't seem to relax. Perhaps… No… I'll never go that far, just gotta stick with weed, everything else is off limits. Speaking of weed, where is that order I had made?

"JJ!" I shout, a little shocked by the anger in my voice but choose to ignore it.

There's a few strands of hair on her shoulders and my eyes go wide when I see it, her hair, her long, brown, luscious hair that she had decided to never cut again back in like 4th grade, all gone, down to a short-cut that makes her look like a grown man.

She frowns upon seeing me, hunched over my bong, skinny and pale. I haven't seen her smile in years, I can't even remember what she looked like smiling. "Where the fuck is the weed I told you to go out and grab?"

"Tyler, I-"

"Don't you start," I cut her off, slamming my bong on the table next to the motel bed. "What did you do with the money I gave you then?"

A dark shadow grows behind her with a sickening grin, great, it's back again. I swear, ever since that day this damn thing has been following me around. Yet whenever I'd bring it up my old bandmates would call me crazy and JJ The Stuck-Up Bitch would suggest cutting me off from the only thing that brought me peace. Fucking bitch, wants everyone to be just as on edge as her at all times. Didn't even bother to at least try some to know what I was experiencing. Then had the nerve to kick me in the nuts when I attempted to give her an edible. Like, seriously? I was just trying to help, bitch.

"I…" She lowers her gaze down to the ground again and I can't help but roll my eyes, "I'm sorry, I'll go get it now."

She quickly grabs her purse and starts to head out the door, "Yeah that's what I thought, you fucking slut." The door slams and I contain myself from going out and yelling at her.

Instead, I just grab my bong and take another puff, ignoring that shadow that's now towering over me.

But it's no use, it's distracting me and is making it impossible to relax. So I turn and stare at it dead in the eye. It is huge, about twice my size, but immensely skinny. It has sharp claws for hands, sharp teeth circling its mouth and eyes that remind me of a snake.

"Won't you just fuck off already."

"She won't come back, you know." The voice is scratchy, and feels as though it is everywhere and nowhere at the same time.

"The bitch fucking better, I gave her the last of my savings."

"The savings from back when you were a lead singer and guitarist, back before you ruined her life."

"Ruined her life? Oh please, if anything she ruined mine by not choosing to smoke with me." I punch the wall, no clue what had gone over me, but I just needed to release. Whatever, it's her fault. "Maybe I'd actually have some more respect for her and forgive her if she'd just sit down and smoke with me."

"Is it because you need a new smoking buddy to ruin the life of?"

"Shut up."

"Like Kyle and Henry, they tried to even help you clean up."

"Shut up."

"Until you killed them."

"I didn't kill anyone!" I launch up to my feet and face the shadow head on. "Those are all just lies!"

"You can't lie to yourself," The shadow laughs. "One became a vegetable and the other overdosed, all because you can't control your weak little mind."

"I did nothing to them! They did it to themselves!"

"Oh? Then how about this?" A needle. But where did it come from? No, I know where it came from, but I refuse to acknowledge it. "You're ready to begin the spiral just like the both of them any day now. Though, unlike Henry, you at least won't have a family and kids to break the hearts of."

"But I won't."

"Yes you will."

"No. I. Won't!" I throw my fists but of course, I only hit air and end up falling onto the cheap, stained mattress.

"You know, you're in this situation all because you just wouldn't listen to- what did her name used to be? Jess? Jessy? Oh but of course you had to ruin her reputation, making her change it to JJ and throw her life away."

"Shut up." My voice is muffled on the mattress, I can't seem to move.

"Does, "22-Year-Old Co-Singer, Jess Burnham, Found Providing Band Members With Several Pounds of Illegal Drugs, Leading to the Downfall of Famous Metal Band 'Kin Slayers' ring a bell?"

"No."

"Are you sure? Because it was posted everywhere, you even provided a quote in it acting as though it was a joke while you were high off your mind."

"No I didn't."

"Oh really, so you didn't tell the entire world on a livestream that she provided you all with the drugs and promoted that you all get high and relax?"

"Shut up."

"That's what I thought."

"What do you even want from me? Clearly I'm just a failure and a junkie in your eyes so what's the point in even acknowledging me?"

"Well, you're not quite the majority's idea of a junkie."

"Excuse me?" I can finally manage to pull myself up and once again, that needle is waiting for me. "No. No, no, no. I will never go to that point."

"Hm." The shadow moves to the other end of the room, entering the bathroom, in a flourish and my heart sinks as I watch it hover over the shit-stained toilet. "Then get rid of it."

"But-but-but it was expensive!"

"Why did you buy it in the first place then?" The shadow, no, the monster grins.

"I-" I stop myself, searching through my memories and possible reasoning but I can't find any likely excuse. "I don't know."

My vision is engulfed in darkness once again, with the only thing in my view being that damn needle. "Then use it, it's not like you have the courage and perseverance to quit weed."

"There's nothing wrong with weed! It's the only drug that is perfectly safe!"

"You're addicted."

"Weed isn't addictive! I can quit anytime!"

"Then why did you never even attempt? Even as you've lost all of your savings, career, gave up on your dream just to smoke yourself stupid, and so, so much more."

Numb. That's how I feel. It's true, I'm just a waste of space—chasing a feeling and destroying everyone in my path. I'm so pathetic, I'll end up dying alone.

"Might as well do what everyone suspects you of." It hovers closer to me, I eye it, the contents inside, the tip of the needle. It's just another step to finally feel calm and happy. That's all. I refuse to say that I'm addicted; because I'm not.

I take it, and begin tapping at my forearm, searching for a vein. Then, as it rises up, I stab it and begin pushing.

"That's right, push it all in, all of it. This is what you're meant to do and you know there's no escape from it."

It's empty. The needle hits the ground. I lay back. And release. I don't know if I've always had an addictive personality, perhaps it's just genetic. Heh, that explains why my parents would limit my sweets consumption back when I was like twelve. Those were the days.

But I know that this is what people expect of me, and there's no point in doing anything else. I'm sorry, Jess, but I couldn't keep my promise. I hope you can forgive me. If you do ever choose to come back, of course.

Goodbye, Henry, Kyle, Jess, Mom, Dad, all of my adoring fans, goodbye.

Complete Fantastical Logic

One month, that's all the time that remains until the museum shuts down with all of the contents inside either being transferred to a new museum or tossed, burned, forgotten. Museums have been closing down left and right ever since The Religious took over, putting an end to history jobs left and right. And my sector, palaeontology, have quite possibly faced the most backlash and cuts ever since the change. Even with literal bones as proof they refuse to believe that there was a time before humans, evolution? Impossible. Dinosaurs? Complete childish fantasy. Even with the current animals and populations actively evolving they still say that it's all false, indoctrinating their children to go against religion. Saying that we're all sick in the head, meanwhile they're pushing the reality of a god while they've never actually physically seen one. 'Oh but I've felt him,' bullshit, you're telling yourself that you felt him just cause you feel sorry for yourself and want to fit in.

Worst part is, a majority of the people are following the belief of the new leaders, even the people who had once fought against them. Now, the only people who are not blinded by the fear of what will happen to them, are the scientists, historians, archeologists, everyone who has seen reality first hand. But we've been silenced. Fired. Even murdered.

I had spent my entire life studying dinosaurs and bones; hell, the cake for my fifth birthday party was even dinosaur themed and I tore that thing apart till I was confident I had collected every last chocolate and gummy bone. My parents had to do a ton of apologising that day, but I didn't care, and still don't to this day. Just like how I don't care what I have to destroy like my past 5-year-old self, I will tear down every single Religious person and barrier in my way till the truth is revealed.

And I know just how to do it.

The first museum I ever worked at is as tall as it is long, and is scheduled to be the last destroyed due to protective laws and all of the reserving and planning that would have to be taken care of in order to ensure every last bit of history and fact is abolished. Good thing processes take forever, no matter what government is in charge.

But even then, it's still just a month left and I highly doubt they will accept delays of any kind. So I have to do this as fast as possible.

Luckily I was able to get my hands on a copy of the keys, the janitor and I were buddies back in the day and was more than willing to give me his set. Other than the tons of boxes and dust and several paintings and statues being taken off of their pedestals, this place is basically the complete same as it was over forty years ago. But I know that there is just one thing within this building that I really truly need to hope hasn't been packed away or burned just yet.

The scroll in the basement.

The red lights overhead do not make it easy to keep my cool, I may be a scientist, and a grown man at that, but red everywhere combined with dark shadows and a ton of dead things can still manage to make me terrified at every turn. But I must muster through, for the sake of science and reality. The sharp teeth on the skull of the tyrannosaurus rex, its devilish grin and lop-sided build that could easily crush me. And due to all museums being shut down with anyone entering facing a punishment as light as ten years in prison I sincerely doubt I'd be found before death greets me and my body joins that of the dinosaurs.

The building is cold, as if ghosts covering every centimetre of this dying place. And each piece of art, bone and lead painting alike, takes me back to when I was just a young man fresh out of university; in love with history and dinosaurs. Working here had even inspired me to write my research paper back when I was getting my PhD. The cracks in the walls from reckless transport men; the chipped paint; the cobwebs and dust in every corner that no janitor could reach; all of it makes me feel young and bright eyed once again. It all reignites a fire within me, one that reassures me that I can't back down till The Religious has been abolished.

I march past the old corner I used to hide away and eat my lunches, still cracked and dark, in an area that nobody bothers to go by. It was sad, I know, but I've always felt comfortable in that tight little area between the dinosaur exhibit and the cafeteria. The floors creak and walls echo as I continue forward, not needing to read the signs up above to know where I'm going. They wouldn't have moved it. In fact, I doubt anyone that has worked here other than a few heads even know it exists. The fascinating scent of old still permeates the entire building, which I've always known to love and accept. Almost as though it is out of my control I run my hands along the black, white, and gold marble walls ignoring the dust that collects on my fingertips.

My hand then runs over a button and the heavy metal door to my right begins to slowly open and I'm soon met with a dark, steep, musky staircase.

Each step creaks as I carefully make my way down, scanning my surroundings with the little vision I have in this pitch black area. It's not long before I'm halfway down, still terrified that I'll tumble and break my neck. It feels as though the walls are closing in, preparing to squish and ferment me till I'm oil. The coarse stone and wood all around me makes me feel stuffy and forces my eyes to water.

I trip on the final step but manage to catch myself on a wall nearby and begin feeling around for a loose brick. Memorising each slight indent and crevice. Each scar that adds a bit of history to this Earth. Until, I finally find it.

With all my strength, I push onto the brick that has an indent of a building and immediately take a step back, blocking my nose and closing my eyes. Can't let the fumes like last time send me to the emergency room.

After about a minute or two of silently waiting off to the side of the entrance I enter the cavern. The flame in the centre is still there, as red and bright as ever, illuminating the entirety of this small area.

And that's when I see it. The scroll on the other side of the room, still stained and preserved in dust. Untouched.

"Perfect," my voice chokes out and I begin to cough, trying to not breathe in the air. With no hesitation, I bolt straight for the scroll, ignoring the hundreds of other artefacts and books. I don't bother checking for booby traps before grabbing onto it, I know this place like the back of my hand and if there were any then I would've set them off years ago.

Blowing and dusting off the paper, I begin carefully unravelling, ignoring my racing heart and shaking hands. Manoeuvring myself and the paper against firelight, I allow my eyes to fall upon the symbols and words before me. This scroll—it will help make everything okay once again. Scientists, historians, everyone and everything will go back to normal. And those damn Religious freaks will no longer have control over us. Hell, I could even try to make it so then scientists are in charge, that way we can completely abolish religion and the world will only remain in pure, unfiltered, facts.

"With a breath and a tap of the heels,
a word shall be uttered,
the eyes will open,
the eyes will glow,
but fear of such will not remain,
the word will be true,
and the truth will be untouched,
time will change,
and all for a price of what is left."

Everyday I get hundreds of messages from people telling me that I've messed up, that I've ruined the world just because I couldn't wait four years. But they're the ones that are wrong, it has been eight years since that day and I couldn't be happier. All of my dreams came true, religion was abolished and only logic had remained. Sure, that sweet neighbour of mine from down the street that just wanted everyone to love each other became a raging bitch, but you know what? Perhaps religion was the root cause of that in everybody already.

Though now that I think about it, a lot of the nice people I've met before that were religious became asses. They had even helped and supported me through my PhD. Hell, they were quite possibly the embodiment of what religion should've been, love, kindness, and peace.

Perhaps I did mess up—

"Nah, I'm retiring next week as a millionaire," I laugh to myself, sipping on a glass of champagne while I relax by the beach, listening as my grandkids run around and play. "I wouldn't trade this even for world peace."

Just In Case

The lights flicker overhead as I enter the gas station in the middle of nowhere, it's sketchy but it's the only stop I had for the next twenty miles. The beeping reminds me of my hangover and I speed walk to one of the pathetic coffee stations in a far corner. Coffee, snacks, gas, that's all I need, just grab that and then book it out of here. No need to answer any unrequired questions, no need to engage in any polite chatter.

Except I didn't think this part through; there are tons of snacks and I have no clue what I want to pick. I could go for the chips, but I can't stand the saltiness not to mention all of the trans fats. I could go for a protein bar but that'll make me fat, and I can't possibly allow that. I could go for a banana but who the hell does that?

A grain bar, that's good enough, it'll create a fuck ton of crumbs but whatever, I'll deal with them later. Next up, the coffee station, stained and repulsive as it is, I still need it in order to dull this hangover as much as possible. And also to keep me awake in this late hassle of a night.

I really can't stand these sorts of places; not only has a giant, brainless, muscle-head of a red neck just come in but he keeps on eyeing me up and down as well. I swear, I might as well buy a pack of smokes just to light them up and chuck them at him. But the act of purchasing them alone isn't good for my image so I'll have to just try to keep my cool and my distance from him. Who knows what those brainless beasts are thinking.

Just like what were the previous people here thinking when they decided to overflow the coffee drip tray and cover the entire counter in shit-brown stains? I gaze around me at the sugar packs and creamers to my left, and a sign to my right on potential deals people could go for if they buy six coffees and trade their first born child.

I'm just kidding.

It's actually after they buy five.

But hey, at least it's any size they want.

I manage to find a large cup that isn't covered in gunk and potential viruses then proceed to place the flimsy round piece of cardboard underneath the espresso spout and watch as it chokes, gages, and farts out the dark, cheap nectar that will keep me going for the next several hours.

"I should also mix in some other crap with it," I mumble to myself, hoping nobody had overhead my deep voice while I scan all of the available cappuccino and latte flavours. Guess I could also toss in a mixture of French vanilla and the 'limited time' pumpkin spice. Whatever, the more caffeine the better.

"How about I provide you with some-" He's behind me. Damn it. I knew I should've brought my pocket knife in with me and judging by how high the shelves are, I doubt the clerk can tell how close he is standing to me, his disgusting breath pressing against my hair. I'd just finished getting it done too. "Assistance."

It's okay. Just keep your cool. Just take a deep breath and try to ignore his horrendous musk. Stay calm. Smile, squint, do what you need to do to keep him off your back without risking him losing his temper.

Taking a step forward and turning to smile at him, I shake my head, "I appreciate it but no thank you, I just enjoy speaking to myself."

That's right, just stay calm and act friendly.

Turning halfway back to my drink, keeping the man in the corner of my eye, I take the cup off of the drink machine and begin searching for a lid. But even with my eyes scanning high and low, I can't seem to find a single lid among the desolate, stained covered section until- Oh thank god, there's one in the back. I reach over to grab the lid, hastily trying to grab it due to no longer having the man within range of sight but I know I've messed up. I'm short, and so had to step up onto my tippy toes.

I hate the feel of his hands on me. What makes him think he can grab my hips, or even touch me for that instance? Oh just because I was bent over the counter and smiled at him? That's why? Go fuck yourself to the moon and don't even bother coming back you waste of fucking air.

But breathe, just breathe, stay calm, don't speak too loud otherwise you'll startle the meat head.

After grabbing the lid and coming back down, I gently remove his hands from my body and ask as femininely as possible, "Excuse me," Activate puppy dog eyes—mean expressions will scare the pinhead, "Can you please not touch me like that? It makes me extremely uncomfortable."

"Oh you know you like it when I touch you," He grabs lower down and my blood begins to boil. "Like how about right here?" He grips onto my vagina and laughs with his putrid breath exhaling onto my neck.

That's it. Fuck all those people online that are like, 'oh just be nice and ask them to stop,' 'oh, make sure to not be mean or rude to them otherwise they'll be very upset and it'll be all your fault.' Fuck all of them. You know what?

In the deepest voice I can muster, I look him dead in the eye and ask, "How's my rocket? My absolute missile? My long, round, girthy eggplant?" I watch as his eyes go wide and he hastily removes his hands, face filled with horror. "Hey, why'd you stop? You seemed to have been enjoying gripping onto my long, hard, veiny, throbbing-"

"Shut up, you fucking freak," His face twitches and it appears that he wants to swing at me but ultimately decides not to as he turns on his heels and books it out of the door.

The commotion has caused quite a bit of people to turn and stare at me with confusion, but luckily none of them heard me speak, so I'm still safe. Just gotta grab my coffee, purchase my snack, and do minimal talking in order to get some more gas in my tank. Perhaps I should grab a lighter as well—just in case.

Comfort Cabin

It was a chilly winter's evening, and the quaint little town of Willowbrook was covered in a soft blanket of snow. The streets were empty, and the only sounds that could be heard were the gentle crunch of boots on fresh snow and the distant laughter of children playing in the park. Nestled on the corner of Elm Street with various vines and plants giving it a nature-y welcome, there stood a charming little hot chocolate shop known as "Comfort Cabin."

Comfort Cabin was no ordinary hot chocolate shop; it was a place where magic happened, where the warmth of friendship and the sweetness of dreams came to life in every cup of hot chocolate they served. The shop was adorned with twinkling fairy lights, cozy armchairs, and bookshelves filled with well-worn classics. It was the perfect escape from the harsh winter outside.

Inside, behind the counter, was Amelia, a young woman with a heart as warm as the hot chocolate she brewed. Her long auburn hair framed a friendly face, and her eyes sparkled with a special kind of kindness. She had inherited Comfort Cabin from her grandmother, who had started it decades ago. Amelia cherished the shop's history and the generations of townsfolk who had found solace within its walls.

As the sun dipped below the horizon, the shop's windows filled with a soft, inviting glow, drawing in weary travellers and locals alike. The bell above the door jingled as it swung open, and in walked Sarah, a teenager bundled up in a cozy scarf and mittens. She was a regular at Comfort Cabin, drawn not just by the hot chocolate but also by the comfort of the place.

Amelia greeted her with a warm smile. "Hey, Sarah! The usual today?"

Sarah nodded, and Amelia began her magic. She took a mug, carefully selected the perfect chocolate blend, and stirred it with love and care. The steam rising from the cup carried the rich aroma of chocolate that filled the air, creating an atmosphere of pure bliss.

Sarah took a seat in her favourite corner, where the armchair was extra cushiony, and a soft blanket was draped over it. She watched as the snowflakes danced outside the window, her heartwarming with every sip. The hot chocolate was more than just a drink; it was a comforting embrace, a taste of childhood, and a respite from the worries of the world.

As Sarah enjoyed her hot chocolate, the doorbell jingled once again, announcing the arrival of Mr. Thompson, the town's old bookseller. He had a stack of old tomes in one hand and a glint in his eye.

"Good evening, Amelia," he greeted her with a nod.

"Mr. Thompson, how lovely to see you. The usual order?" Amelia asked, already reaching for the book she knew he'd want.

He chuckled, "Of course, the usual."

Amelia handed him a cup of hot chocolate and his preferred book, a tattered copy of "Pride and Prejudice." Mr. Thompson settled into a corner, lost in the world of Jane Austen, while the fire crackled softly in the background.

Comfort Cabin had that effect on people; it was a sanctuary where the troubles of the world faded away, if only for a little while. The warm ambiance, the aroma of chocolate, and the comfort of books worked their magic on anyone who crossed its threshold.

Hours passed, and the shop filled with a gentle hum of conversation and contentment. Friends shared stories over cups of hot chocolate, lovers whispered sweet nothings, and families laughed together. The hot chocolate shop was not just a place for solitude; it was also a place for connection.

As the evening wore on, a young couple entered, their faces flushed from the cold. They were on their first date, nerves evident in their smiles and the way they fidgeted with their scarves.

Amelia noticed their hesitation and decided to play Cupid. She prepared two special hot chocolates, each with a heart-shaped marshmallow floating on top. She served them with a wink and a knowing smile.

The couple blushed but thanked her, and with their hot chocolates in hand, they found a quiet corner. The magic of Comfort Cabin worked wonders, and soon their awkwardness gave way to laughter and shared dreams.

The shop began to empty out, the last customers lingering over their hot chocolates and conversations. Amelia cleaned up, humming a soft tune, grateful for another day of warmth and connections.

As the clock struck midnight, she closed the shop, the bell above the door ringing one final time. She turned off the lights, leaving only the soft glow of the fairy lights, and locked the door behind her.

Walking home through the snow-covered streets, Amelia couldn't help but smile. Comfort Cabin was more than just a hot chocolate shop; it was a place where hearts were warmed, friendships were forged, and dreams were shared—a cozy haven in the heart of winter.

Whispers Of Shadows And Light

In the shadowed realm of Miniroth, where moonlight rarely touched the earth and the air bore a heavy scent of decay, there existed a guild of assassins known as the Nightzalea Brotherhood. Among them was a figure cloaked in darkness, a lethal wraith whose name struck terror into the hearts of those who heard it whispered in the alleys and corridors of the city. They called him Darian Nighkin.

Darian was no ordinary assassin. He moved with the grace of a panther, his every step silent, and his blade swift and merciless. His eyes, cold and calculating, betrayed no emotion as he navigated the twisted streets of Miniroth on his latest assignment. The Nightzalea Brotherhood had been contracted by a mysterious client to eliminate a high-ranking noble who harbored dangerous secrets. The target was said to reside in the sprawling mansion atop the hill, surrounded by twisted trees and hidden in perpetual shadow.

As Darian approached the mansion, he noticed an unusual stillness in the air. The moon, shrouded by thick clouds, cast an eerie glow over the darkened landscape. The mansion loomed like a ghostly sentinel, its windows dark and foreboding. Darian melted into the shadows, becoming one with the night as he scaled the walls and slipped through an open window.

Inside, the mansion was a labyrinth of dimly lit corridors and forgotten chambers. Darian moved with purpose, guided by the whispers of the shadows. He encountered no guards, no obstacles to hinder his progress. It was as if the mansion itself had resigned to its fate.

Finally, Darian reached the door to the noble's private chamber. With a swift and silent motion, he pushed it open and entered. The room was adorned with opulent tapestries and decadent furnishings, a stark contrast to the grim reality of Miniroth. At the center of the room, the noble slept soundly, oblivious to the impending danger.

As Darian raised his blade to strike the fatal blow, a sudden burst of light filled the room. Startled, he recoiled, his eyes squinting against the sudden radiance. When he opened them again, he was met with a sight that defied the laws of his dark world.

An angel stood before him, her wings bathed in celestial light. Her presence radiated warmth and purity, a stark contrast to the cold darkness that clung to Darian. She looked at him with eyes that held the wisdom of the ages, and yet, beneath the serenity, there was a glint of something untamed.

"You are not like the others," she spoke, her voice a melodic harmony that echoed through the chamber.

Darian, caught off guard by the ethereal being before him, found himself unable to respond. His blade, poised for the kill, trembled in his grasp.

"I have watched you, Darian Nighkin," the angel continued. "You are not as heartless as your reputation suggests. There is a flicker of humanity within you, a longing for something more."

Darian, a man of few words, remained silent. He watched the angel, uncertain of what to make of this unexpected encounter.

"I have been sent to deliver a message," the angel said. "Your path is not set in stone. There is a choice before you, a chance for redemption. Love has the power to transform even the darkest soul."

Love. The word echoed in the stillness of the room, a concept foreign to Darian. He had long believed himself beyond such trivial emotions, a creature of the night bound by duty and darkness.

As if sensing his internal struggle, the angel extended a hand towards him. "Come, Darian. Embrace the light within you. There is someone who awaits your redemption, someone whose fate is entwined with yours."

Against his better judgment, Darian found himself drawn to the angel's outstretched hand. As their fingers touched, a surge of warmth coursed through him, and a vision unfolded before his eyes.

He saw her—a woman with eyes that held both vulnerability and strength. A woman who moved through the shadows with the same fluid grace as him, her purpose veiled in mystery. In that moment, Darian realized the angel spoke of more than mere redemption. She spoke of love, a force that could break the chains of his dark existence.

The vision faded, and Darian stood alone in the noble's chamber, the weight of his choices pressing upon him. The angel's presence lingered, a gentle whisper in the recesses of his mind.

The next night, Darian found himself wandering the desolate streets of Miniroth, his thoughts consumed by the encounter with the angel. The city seemed darker, colder, as if the shadows themselves recoiled from the internal turmoil that raged within him.

As he moved through the twisted alleys, a figure emerged from the darkness—a woman with eyes that mirrored the vision he had seen. She was clad in shadows, a silhouette against the inky night.

"Darian Nighkin," she spoke, her voice a velvet whisper. "I've been waiting for you."

Darian, normally composed and unflinching, felt a knot tighten in his chest. This woman, the one whose fate was entwined with his, stood before him. Her name was Alara, and she was a fellow assassin who operated in the murky depths of Miniroth.

"I saw you in a vision," Darian admitted, his voice betraying a vulnerability he had never known.

Alara's eyes softened, and she stepped closer. "I saw you too. There's something different about you, Darian. As if the shadows that cloaked you have begun to wane."

Darian hesitated, torn between the darkness that had defined him and the glimmer of light that beckoned from within. He recounted the encounter with the angel, the choice that lay before him.

"Love," Alara mused, a hint of a smile playing on her lips. "A powerful force, indeed. Perhaps it's time we embraced the light together."

In the weeks that followed, Darian and Alara navigated the treacherous terrain of their dual lives as assassins. They faced danger at every turn, their enemies closing in on the fragile sanctuary they had built in the heart of Miniroth.

As their love deepened, so too did the shadows that sought to consume them. The mysterious client who had once employed Darian now turned his attention to the rogue assassins who dared defy the natural order of Miniroth. The couple found themselves hunted by former allies, their every move shadowed by the looming threat of death.

In the midst of the chaos, the angel appeared once more, her presence a guiding light in their darkest hour. She spoke of a prophecy that foretold a union between a creature of shadows and one touched by the divine. Together, Darian and Alara held the power to bring balance to Miniroth or plunge it into eternal darkness.

The final confrontation unfolded in the same mansion where Darian had once stood poised to end a life. Now, the noble's chamber became the battleground for a clash of fates. The angel watched from the shadows as Darian and Alara faced the forces that sought to tear them apart.

The former allies, now turned adversaries, encircled the couple. Blades clashed, and shadows danced in a macabre symphony of violence. Darian moved with the skill of a master assassin, his every strike calculated and deadly. Beside him, Alara fought with a fierce determination, her movements a deadly ballet that defied the conventions of the underworld.

In the midst of the chaos, the mysterious client revealed himself—a sorcerer whose lust for power drove him to manipulate the threads of destiny. He sought to harness the dark energy that coursed through Darian and the divine light that emanated from Alara to achieve godlike status.

As the battle raged on, the angel descended from the shadows, her wings unfurling in a radiant display of celestial power. With a gesture, she unleashed a surge of energy that dispelled the darkness that clung to the sorcerer. In that moment, Darian and Alara felt a surge of power within themselves, a union of shadow and light that transcended the boundaries of their individual beings.

With newfound strength, they faced the sorcerer together. Darian's blade met the sorcerer's dark magic, while Alara's shadows wove a protective barrier around them. The battle reached its climax as the sorcerer unleashed his most potent spell, a vortex of swirling shadows and blinding light.

In that crucible of chaos, Darian and Alara embraced, their love forming a shield that defied the sorcerer's malevolent magic. The angel, her eyes ablaze with divine power, joined their union, and together they shattered the sorcerer's ambitions.

As the dust settled, Miniroth emerged from the grip of darkness. The twisted city, once bound by the shadows, now basked in the dappled light of a rejuvenated moon. The Nightzalea Brotherhood disbanded, their allegiance shattered by the revelation that love could triumph over the darkest of destinies.

Darian and Alara, their love forged in the crucible of chaos, stood at the precipice of a new beginning. The angel, her purpose fulfilled, ascended to the heavens, leaving behind a city that had been forever changed by the union of an assassin and an angel.

Together, Darian and Alara vowed to rebuild their lives, no longer bound by the shadows that had defined them. Love had become their guiding light, a force that transcended the boundaries of their pasts and illuminated a future where darkness and light could coexist in harmony. And so, hand in hand, they walked into the uncertain dawn, their destinies intertwined in a tale that defied the conventions of Miniroth's dark fantasy.

Cyn-mas

In a nondescript town enveloped by snow, Victor Granger, known for his perpetual cynicism, found himself at the local pub on Christmas Eve, seeking refuge from the festive fervour outside. The bar was adorned with typical holiday decorations, but Victor paid little mind. Christmas, in his book, was just another day. And he often hated the ads that came along with it. So joyful, colourful, wasteful.

As the clock struck midnight, a mysterious figure entered, bearing a peculiar gift—an old-fashioned pocket watch. The stranger, in a long, dark coat and wearing a mask painted with the snow that blocks their face, claimed it could reveal life's beauty, even in Victor's most cynical moments. Nonsense. Victor, always sceptical, accepted the watch with a scoff and tossed it into his pocket without a second thought. Contemplating tossing it down a drain somewhere, or perhaps chucking it into the yard of an orphanage, just wait and see how beautiful those poor kids' faces will be when they realise how trapped they really are. No amount of cheap, petty grocery store gifts will change anything.

Exiting the pub, Victor wandered through the snowy streets, the watch beginning to emit a soft glow. Unbeknownst to him, an enchantment unfolded. A patch of black ice yielded from seemingly out of nowhere, and Victor found himself face-first on the ground, his world fading to black.

When he awoke, disoriented and with no recollection of who he was, Victor discovered the mysterious pocket watch still in his possession. It glowed softly, guiding him through the town, revealing fragments of a past he couldn't remember. Or perhaps didn't bother to.

As he interacted with townsfolk who claimed to know him, Victor struggled to reconcile the person they described with the cynical man he knew himself to be. The watch led him to scenes of kindness and joy – helping neighbours, playing with children, and even participating in a Christmas choir. Victor couldn't fathom that this alternate version of himself existed.

He couldn't figure out if this was for certain his past, or perhaps a whole 'nother dimension, or maybe the watch was just laced with fentanyl. Typical.

Or maybe not.

Being shown pictures of old, upon peoples' phones of himself. The laughing, light-hearted memories, and the kind faces, offering their extra pairs of mittens or to join them for a coffee run. Victor can't help but find himself feeling, almost at home. Safe even. But how? Why?

Throughout the day, Victor's heart softened. The pocket watch offered him a glimpse of a life he had never imagined. He began to appreciate the warmth of the people around him and the simple pleasures of the holiday season. The once-cynical man found himself immersed in the magic of Christmas. Or fentanyl, you never know.

As midnight approached, the mysterious figure reappeared, revealing themselves to be a familiar face. The hood fell back, exposing a knowing smile.

"Do you understand now, Mr. Granger?" the stranger asked.

Victor, a mix of emotions within him, nodded. "I never knew... I never realised."

The stranger explained the watch's power to temporarily erase memories, offering individuals a chance to rediscover life without the burdens of their past. Victor had been chosen to experience this enchantment, learning that even the most cynical heart could be transformed by the spirit of Christmas.

But what had caused Victor to be so damn cynical?

As the clock struck midnight once again, Victor's memories returned. The lessons of that magical Christmas Eve stayed with him. The pocket watch became a symbol of transformation, a cherished reminder that even the coldest hearts can thaw in the magic of the holiday season.

From that day forward, Victor Granger became a changed man. He embraced the joy, love, and kindness around him, participating in community events and spreading the warmth he had discovered during his amnesiac Christmas adventure. The pocket watch, now an heirloom, served as a reminder that second chances and newfound perspectives can emerge, even for those who believe they've seen it all.

Even for those who faced traumas of failed relationships, loss of homes, and loss of loved ones can still eventually find joy even in the darkest places of their minds.

Veiled Blade

The howling winds of the dark, desolate landscape whipped through the tattered cloak of Sir Dorian Blackhorn, once a hero amongst his people, now condemned to wander as an exile. His name, once synonymous with honour and valour, was now whispered with disdain and fear. Loathing. Dorian's eyes, steel-grey and weathered by the storms of betrayal, scanned the barren horizon as he rode through the unfamiliar land that offered neither solace nor respite.

It had all unravelled with the malevolent tearing of the earth—a great chasm ripping apart the land like a bleeding wound. Demons, born of black blood formed by dark magic and unleashed by the nefarious machinations of the court mage, poured forth like a relentless tide, devouring all in their path. Sir Dorian had been charged with leading the king's army and defending the empire, but nothing in his storied past could have prepared him for this cataclysm.

From the window of his once-grand chamber, Dorian had watched in helpless horror as the empire crumbled under the onslaught of the demonic horde. The court mage, a twisted man with a penchant for forbidden arts, was behind it all. His experiments with necromancy had crossed the boundaries of what was natural and holy, tearing the veil between worlds and unleashing an unholy menace upon the realm. No soul was safe from his demented breaths, not even that of new born children, children that have not even been scarred with the deaths of their mothers.

Determined to rectify the chaos and save his people, Dorian stormed into the royal court with conviction burning in his veins. His armour clanked with each step, and the hilt of his sword echoed his determination. But the mage was already there, an insidious smile playing on his lips.

"There he is, my king," the mage proclaimed wickedly, pointing an accusing finger at Dorian. "The one who unleashed hell. Guards, kill him!"

The king, bewildered and desperate for a scapegoat, looked upon the once-heroic general with suspicion. In that moment, Dorian realised the gravity of the betrayal—his efforts to expose the true culprit had been in vain. And no amount of begging could help the ones around him perceive the truth. The king, swayed by the mage's manipulative words, had deemed Dorian the architect of the empire's downfall.

The royal guards, loyal to their sovereign, drew their weapons with a reluctant yet determined resolve. Dorian, betrayed and cornered, fought his way out of the castle, his sword cutting down those he had once called comrades. Blood stained the polished marble floors as he made his escape, leaving behind the shattered remnants of his former life. Of any chance of love, freedom, and truth.

The journey through deserts and mountains had been gruelling, each step a painful reminder of the once-revered knight's fall from grace. The burden of the prince's blood on his hands weighed heavily on Dorian's conscience, a perpetual reminder of the choices forced upon him. With each passing day, the memories of his home became a bittersweet ache, a fading echo of what once was. His childhood, now burned up behind him, with the truth gaslit into darkness like the embers of a fireplace, being smothered till all that is left is a final exhale.

Eventually, after weeks of relentless riding, Dorian found himself in a foreign land, an unforgiving expanse that held neither sympathy nor judgement. The faces of the people were unfamiliar, and the languages spoken were foreign to his ears. A stranger in a strange land, Dorian knew he must start anew, shedding the identity of the fallen hero and embracing the cold pragmatism of survival.

In the shadow of towering mountains, Dorian sought refuge in a nondescript, snowy village. The air was thick with the scent of unfamiliar spices and the chatter of a language he could barely comprehend. Despite the foreign surroundings, Dorian observed the familiar aspects of human nature—the hustle and bustle of marketplaces, the laughter of children playing, and the companionship of a community bound by shared struggles. Perhaps struggles caused by frequent raids, disease, and loss.

Desperation became Dorian's companion as he sought out any means to survive in this alien realm. His once-shining armour was traded for nondescript clothing, and the renowned Blackhorn sword became a tool of anonymity, hidden beneath layers of cloth. Dorian offered his skills as a seasoned warrior to the highest bidder, taking on tasks that ranged from escorting caravans through treacherous terrain to dealing with local bandit threats. But he never so as complained, no matter how gruesome and tiring, he never complained about what he had left—for it was still much better than being locked up, tortured, and spat on by the ones he'd once called family.

In the face of adversity, Dorian discovered a latent pragmatism within himself, adapting to the harsh realities of his new existence. The once-champion of justice and honour now navigated the murky waters of morally ambiguous contracts, the lines between right and wrong blurred by the necessity of survival. The echoes of his past life haunted him, but Dorian found solace in the anonymity of his new identity—a man without a past, surviving in the shadows. Making a living one job, one task, one mission at a time.

As the seasons changed and the years passed, Dorian honed his skills as a master tactician and a formidable warrior. His reputation as a sellsword spread across the land, drawing the attention of those in need of a blade skilled enough to carve through adversity. In the dimly lit taverns where whispers of treachery and betrayal circulated like the smoke from a hundred pipes, Dorian found his purpose.

One fateful evening, as the sun dipped below the horizon and the village was shrouded in shadows, a hooded figure approached Dorian. The stranger's eyes glinted with an intensity that betrayed a hidden purpose. In a voice that resonated with secrets, the mysterious figure spoke. Crisp and dry.

"Sir Dorian Blackhorn, once a hero, now a shadow in the tapestry of time. I have a proposition for you."

Dorian's gaze locked with the enigmatic stranger, curiosity and caution warring within him. The figure unveiled a parchment adorned with an intricate seal—a sigil that hinted at clandestine dealings and concealed power.

"I represent an organisation that seeks to restore balance to the realms," the stranger explained. "We are aware of your past, the injustices thrust upon you. Join us, and together we shall uncover the truth behind the malevolent forces that tore your world asunder."

The words hung in the air, pregnant with the promise of redemption and vengeance. Over the years, Dorian thought that perhaps he would've turned down the possibility of going back, if the offer ever arose—content with what he had made of him. But now with the option in front of him, he honestly doesn't even know what he wants himself. Dorian, torn between the memories of his former life and the pragmatism that had become his shield, felt a spark of hope. The shadow of exile began to lift, replaced by the possibility of a new purpose.

With a nod, Dorian accepted the stranger's proposition. The wheels of fate, once set into motion by betrayal and despair, now creaked with the weight of a hero's redemption. The path ahead was uncertain, but in the darkness, Dorian Blackhorn found a glimmer of light—a chance to reclaim his honour and face the demons that had haunted him since that fateful day.

Disciple Two : A Shrouded Personas Short Story

Today's the day: the day of my first ever solo mission. After nine whole years of hardened training, sensory enlightenment, and leadership coordination, I'm finally allowed to travel and finish a job all on my own. Sadly, I'm not the youngest to have ever been allowed to do so, but compared to the kids at my day school, I should still be quite proud. I guess. Ulea, the underwater nation, high tech, rich, mostly snobby. I have a lot to work on within the next eight hours till I depart, especially when it comes to trying to fit in. So best to start doing my research now. I have the whole weekend, till Sunday night, to be able to finish whatever task that will be assigned to me.

Sadly I have to get through this field trip first. Luckily it involves swimming, so I can get some practice with deep diving. My skinny body has always made it difficult to get very deep–usually resulting in me just bouncing back up–so this time will be good for me. As long as I'm not forced to work with any of these hooligans or do set swimming practices. Hopefully the pool is big enough for me to get my own lane, or at least a section in the deep end to practise. But alas, it's a trip with seventy-six other kids and a whole 'nother school, so chances are slim that I'll even have enough space to breathe.

But no matter, I can work my way around it and find a way to practise, I always do.

Until then, I have to get through this awful carriage ride. We've been assigned as eight kids a carriage, when it only seats four, maximum, and I'm currently stuck between a boy who hasn't showered since first snowfall–it's practically spring–and a girl who won't stop scream laughing in my ear whenever her "crush" says something "funny." In reality, she only acts kind towards that blond-haired, blue-eyed imbecile because his birthday is coming up and his family is known for making some of the best homemade cake. I've never got to try it before. It had been brought to school to share with the class a few times but someone would always either take mine or just refuse to give me one altogether. But no matter, sugar is a drug, and I have no intentions to become an overweight addict.

Throughout the hour-long ride I was spoken to twice and spoken about more than seventeen times. None of which were positive. But I don't care, being naive and wanting friends is for weaklings, and I have no intention of dying before my first ever solo mission. I will not cry if these people die gruesome deaths that I could've prevented either. Humans are horrible creatures, and it's quite possible that even the habitants of Kolsant or Sortirid are practically monsters in and of themselves.

"Alright everyone, file out in a line of pairs!" My morning teacher, Mrs. Pritchard, calls out in front of the doors to the massive, primarily-windowed building in front of us. It's shocking really, that a single company, let alone a person, could afford to build and maintain something like this. All that water, now filled with chemicals and undrinkable, just sitting in there, being filled to the brim on a daily basis with a bunch of disgusting, unhygienic, grotesque kids.

I have a choice now, the unshowered pig, or the louder-than-a-fire-alarm girl. One risking my sense of smell, the other, my hearing. Honestly, I'd rather not breathe through my nose for the next few minutes than end up with hearing issues before my mission.

Pig it is.

I choose to tune out all of the chatter, letting it flow to the back of my mind and remain there until there is some information I may need.

Luckily it doesn't take very long till we are all in our gender-designated locker rooms, with soaking wet floors and mud left, right, and centre. For some reason there's even mud in the lockers. But what can you expect? It's a farming nation with dry dirt everywhere, so if you toss in a huge-ass pool then you can expect there to only be mud wherever the eye can see and more.

Sadly there are only about fifty lockers available so not nearly enough for all of us, instead I was offered to leave my bag in one of the instructors' offices and I jumped at it. I don't trust these people. Plenty of things get taken out of unattended bags on a regular basis.

We're supposed to shower up before going into the pool but I don't want to, among many other girls, so we all go straight to the bleachers completely dry. The boys all stare at us, due to some of us being in two-pieces or bikinis, but I ignore them. A few of the girls are nervous or shy and I get the temptation to motivate and encourage them but then choose to think better of it. I've done it before, it did not go well. However, somehow out of all the girls here, I'm one of the few who are completely unshaven and despite not having to worry about being cold, I do, however, need to worry about being stared at and picked on by all of the hideous, smelly, unfathomable boys.

I tune their jabs and insults out though—instead calculating the P.H of the water or the depth or the water pressure and how I can expect it to affect my ears and eyes at the bottom of the pool. I'm not allowed to shave, not until I'm thirteen and have to go on more dangerous missions, ones where I can't risk leaving any DNA behind. For now my school doesn't want us thinking about our bodies other than stamina, strength, speed, basically things that actually help during missions and jobs.

The pool is quite large, eight lanes, can probably fit two and a half kids per lane width, and it gets deeper the further you get. There aren't any high-diving boards, but instead just one diving board right above the water and a few blocks used for speed diving in every other lane. By the looks of it, the water only goes down to thirty feet deep, not the best, but still good for practising I guess. There's a second pool room in the back, judging by the steam in the corners of the windows it must be a hot tub of sorts. It has nets up inside as well so it must be to promote sport play. I don't think I've ever been in a hot tub before, probably when I was a baby and was being given Radical Thermal Training but that was about it.

After a long while, four tall, dark haired women in brown one-pieces come and stand in front of us, placing their fingers on their lips to signal us to be quiet. The tallest one, a dark skinned woman, goes first. "Good morning, our young swimmers, we will be your instructors for today. My name is Natalie Grasse, but you will call me Ms. Grasse. Now, due to you all being of the same swimming level, we will instead be separating by height, starting with the tallest. So everyone, please line up around the pool from tallest to shortest with the tallest being by me and the shortest being by my colleague on the other end named Ms. Grown. Chop, chop."

At an instant everyone gets up and rushes to where they believe they belong, however, even though throughout the entire school it's known that I'm the tallest, many kids still try and line up in front of Ms. Grasse. To which she instantly sees me above all of their heads, gives them serious looks, and silently points them to line up properly.

It's awkward while we wait for everyone to finish lining up around the pool, especially since we also had to wait for all of the instructors to finish their hushed discussion on how many kids will go to which group. It appears that the second school is taking a while to arrive, which for now is good for me since it means more time to practise than wait.

After another long while, the groups are all finally decided and we are all taken to different parts of the pool, the shortest group of which is going straight to the hot tub. Looks like we are going to the hot tub separately.

My group is taken to the deep end of the pool though, sadly, due to all of us being at such a low level, we are all forced to wear life jackets. Damn it. How am I supposed to practise my diving and prepare my ears for the pressure if I can hardly even get past the surface of the water? I guess I could work on my strength in terms of getting through the buoyancy of the jacket. Yeah, that could work.

It didn't work. I tried to get down deep but each and every time the woman dove in and tried to "save" me due to assuming I was drowning. After my eighth attempt I was forced to get dressed and sit on the bleachers, didn't even get to use the hot tub, and my group was sent in the moment I had gotten back from the locker room. They looked like they were having fun, but I doubt I would've enjoyed it. Being stuck in a small back room encased in glass with people playing volleyball in boiling hot water? Pass. At least I had been able to spend the remaining hour and a half here watching the woman show the others how to dive and swim fast, as well as good breathing techniques. I would've preferred to practise them in water, but I'll take what I can get and practice breathing on land.

I was the first to be sent into the carriage due to being dressed already, though sadly that also means I was stuck with one of my teachers, and she was not happy. She would just not stop complaining about how stupid, lazy, and embarrassing of a child I am.

"I swear, you might as well rip off all of your clothes and beg on your knees for the attention of the boys around you," She grumbles through tensed teeth with a fierce glare. "You damn kids nowadays, always just begging for attention by flailing your damn pussies left and right, crying desert."

Ah, projecting.

Poor Ms. Lint, she didn't ask to be completely cut off from her daughters' lives, but she did, however, deserve it. Practically begged for it. And quite literally with her pussy out for her daughters' boyfriends.

It's a long ride back to the old, dusty, straw-like school, the entirety of it being spent with Ms. L lecturing us all on sex and how useless and immature we all are. If I cared then I'd definitely feel bad for the boys, after the fifteenth "pussy" they started to get uncomfortable and that's when she began sexualising them.

Stepping off of that carriage felt similar to escaping a gas chamber and taking my first few actual breaths of air. But now I must focus on my mission, starting off with getting through the next hour of school. Which I don't have to get through cause I refuse to stick around for the rest of the day, one hour or not. I don't care if there's a pizza party waiting for me in there, I refuse to go in and just take it as everyone picks on and tries to fight me cause they're all riled up.

First breath. Second breath. Third breath. And I take off. Heel to toe, heel to toe. Dust kicking up behind me, and each in to exhale being tracked to ensure stability. Arms swaying to keep up with the rhythm. Faster. I need to go faster.

Faster than the ships of Ulea, faster than their steeds, faster than their olympians.

I need to go faster.

But I'm back at my shack before I can manage a new record.

Twenty-five minutes, depressing. I managed nineteen just two weeks ago. I'll need to try harder. But not now. Now I need to rest and save my energy for my trip to Ulea. How long is it till school starts? About three to four hours? Okay, yeah, that's enough time to pack and head over. And then after my first class I should expect to be called out for my mission. My classmates are going to be so jealous. Though the one's who'd gone before me are going to be so stuck up.

Whatever, I can't be thinking about that.

My shack, brown, hints of silver from chipped paint, and made entirely of what most would assume as thick tin-foil, stands before me. With a cracked window, broken wood door slightly ajar, and a sandy pathway leading up, stomped down and begging for fresh rain.

Me too, pathway, me too.

The rocks knock against each other as I make my way up to the front, not bothering to knock, nobody is waiting for me inside. Nobody will ever be waiting for me inside. Nobody has ever waited for me inside.

The door creaks and screams as I nudge it off its hinges, catching it just before it tumbles and squeezing past as I push it against its foil frame once again.

Four hours. That's the amount of time I have until it's time for my night school; that's the amount of time I have until it's time for my mission. My first ever solo mission.

I have to take every second available to me to prepare.

To start, potions. I don't have much available to me, at least with the way the environment has been lately. But I still have little things that improve stamina, weight loss, and even one that can make me slightly transparent. Useless. That's what I am—utterly useless.

No, I can't start downtalking myself now. I've come this far so clearly I must be capable of something. But no matter, I still need to figure out something to do to help me prepare, even if I have to take a run to the library to look up potions. Damn it, I should've paid more attention in my geography and potion classes. Well, more of all my classes, but right now those are the primary ones that would be of use to me.

Come on, think, think, think.

Gazing around the entirety of my shack, one vital task comes to mind. I know.

"Disciple Two, please, make your way to dispatch room A-7E for your upcoming mission to Ulea."

The speakers roar throughout my classroom. They were quick to send me off, perhaps it's because this is a four day job and I only have three days to complete it. But luckily I was able to get through roll call before being sent away.

The class watches with silent, blank stares—portraying nothing of their inner thoughts, of their opinions. But I know what each and every one of them think, each had shown their feelings upon the first reveal of my mission. The ones ahead of me want to laugh and mock me for being after them, the ones who have not yet been chosen wish to take me out as some sort of overrated competitor. But now I at least don't need to worry about them attempting to remove me from the schools' records, the only focus now is succeeding in whatever task I'm about to receive.

The hallways are long, tall, and polished to perfection. Seeming to go on with no end in sight. There is a drinking fountain with an electrolyte and vitamin dispenser on the right corner of the wall I'm about to pass, a smudge of blood on its sensor, likely an older student that had finished a combat class.

There are no decorations on the walls, no colours in sight other than the blood stains. Everything is white, and cold, and silent. Even my footsteps fail to make a noise. My heart is in my throat, thumping as I breathe, focusing on remaining practically invisible. There's no need for me to do this–to hide my presence and be so anxious–but it's good practice, to prove to myself what it is that I am capable of. And to distract myself from the anxiety resulting from my upcoming task.

Some sort of cleaning solution, possibly sodium hypochlorite, that's what the next four hallways smell like. They're for the older kids, fourteen to sixteen so it likely needs to be cleaned far more frequently. I remember smelling a cleaning solution at my school once, it smelled like lemons and was so relaxing. I wish I had spending hungins, that way I could get a bottle of the solution for myself and just spend my down time smelling it. But that would never be allowed due to the risk of it killing my brain cells.

The dispatch rooms are labelled with sheets of metal just above each door.

"A1, A2, A3…" I mumble to myself reading out each of the numbers as I search for mine. "AE, AF, AG…" Millions of dispatch rooms, and with each door I get closer to where I'm supposed to end up. "A-7C, A-7D," I've arrived. "A-7E."

Before I get the chance to knock or scan my prints, the door shoots up and I'm met face-to-face with a tall-looking man boy. His hair is long, dark brown, but tied up into braids that make their way down the back of his head. His skin is dark, possibly from Rapard? He has the glossy eyes that typically come from growing up there. Or perhaps he just goes there frequently for missions. There are bags under his eyes, deep and soulless, like he hadn't slept in weeks or had just watched a loved one die. But that's impossible, loved ones are forbidden. There's a smidge of facial hair on him but his face is also round like a healthy baby, an offsetting combination.

He marches past me before I get a good look at his build and clothing, not bothering to even acknowledge me before setting off down the long, white hallways where I had just come.

"Ah, Disciple Two, you've finally made it."

I turn back towards the door to see a tall, lanky man in a white lab coat and thick, difficult to see through glasses. I scan his nametag, '9803527,' I believe the nine and seven beginning and endings typically mean Child-Experimentation Scientists but at the same time the amount of numbers also matter. Just can't remember if it's supposed to be seven or eight total numbers. But even then, why is an experimentation scientist all the way out here anyway? Is he here for me or that other kid?

"Come in and take a seat, I'll call in the leader meant to give you the rundown." He waves me inside and I follow him down the dark hallway until we finally make it to a large room with a jet and a submarine on the far side and an office on the other. It's decently dark in here but not so bad that I struggle to see where I'm going.

He leads me to the office and holds the door open for me, gesturing for me to take a seat at the large round table in the centre. He then shuts and locks the door and I watch him on the cameras on the TV in the corner of the room as he makes a call and heads out on his way. The office is large, but not overwhelming, the walls are completely white, there's a desk with a thermal chair and two monitors in the corner, covered in papers and files. A black bookshelf just next to the doorway with books that must have thousands of pages each, the TV is just above the desk. In the corner opposite to the desk is a water fountain with a spout with some sort of focusing potion. And then the centre of the room has a large, dark brown round table with ten office chairs going all around it, each neatly pushed in and out of the way.

I don't bother continuing to look around after the initial scan, instead I just stay put, watching the cameras up in the corner as a woman in a lab coat with her hair tied up into a messy bun comes rushing over to the office carrying a file.

The door opens with a hurry and she comes rushing in, moving to take the seat across from me. "Sorry, sorry, so sorry. Things have just been a mess ever since the new import and export laws. I tell you, I haven't gotten even an hour of sleep in total for the past week due to having to research all of the loopholes." She places the file down and takes a seat, then opens it up and begins skimming through it, "Ah, Disciple Two," She says with a deep breath and upbeat smile. She looks much younger when she smiles, perhaps her late twenties. "I see here that you have a mission in Ulea for this weekend, first ever solo one, congratulations." I don't bother smiling, instead remaining silent and professional. "Well, it appears here that this mission is mostly a bounty-hunting kind of job."

Shit, I've never been that good at actively tracking people down. I had always just piggybacked off of my groupmates' experience. And I guarantee with the job being so long that I'll have little to nothing to go off of as well. Maybe I'm not ready for a solo mission just yet. Maybe I should find a way to get out of this and instead take my time to build up wherever I may be lacking.

"And it says here that your compatibility with this job is actually one hundred percent," She takes a few papers out of her pile and passes them over to me. "That's actually pretty amazing, it's not as rare nowadays but back when I was your age, complete matches were basically a once in a blue moon occurrence." She pauses for a moment and laughs to herself, "Wow, that just made me sound so old, and I'm only forty seven."

Forty what now?

I thought she was in her twenties!

But then again, now that I'm taking a closer look, there are quite a lot of wrinkles on her face and hands.

"Alright, so basically you'll be taken to Ulea's main port at Shinshul, we've decided that hiding in plain sight would be best for this job. However, we don't want you to stick out like a sore thumb, so you will be given a few pairs of clothes in their colour which will be burned when you are on your way back. Some will be good for stealth, others for just blending in." I read through the papers, my profile, locations, tips, people, and so on. "Your target is a middle-aged man named Olimpik Senio Kim, he is a notorious child murderer and kidnapper, however even then nobody has been able to spot him. We are not certain but have suspicions that he is white, as white as snow, with either silver, ginger, or black hair, and is below the average height for men in that area–so close-ish to you, perhaps shorter." She then hands me a few pictures of the possible appearance of the man, though due to no other features being known it is instead some blank faces with different colours and styles of hair. "No other details are known at this time. Locations have varied. Hell, we can't even understand what his general goals for targets are other than that they are children–not even an age range."

Silently, I flip through the pages, memorising the information on them. I'll be taken to an inn upon my arrival by the owner–who will be acting as my uncle–who owes the school a favour. There I will be housed, fed, and will find the rest of my clothing. The owner requests that I have little to no interactions with him during my stay, reasonable. I'll be taken to the port via the transforming submarine that will be led by a student in training. It's recommended that little to no weapons are revealed during my job, however, stealth needles will be provided for safety purposes. There will be two small sacks, one will be laced with a powerful tranquilliser, the other a form of psychedelic. So far the man has claimed an estimate of fifteen victims within the last two weeks. The media has been working hard to cover up the missing children until I return from my mission in order to ensure there is no one who wishes to intervene.

Alright, it appears that they covered everything to make up for the very little that is known, which is good. Though I just wish I had a bit more to work with in terms of appearance, or at least voice, mannerisms, something.

"You will also be given a communication device in the ship, this is just to tell us if you had forgotten anything, that way we can transport it to you without risk of raising any attention. It will vapourize exactly one hour after your arrival to the inn, so be sure to unpack quickly." She adds with a cautiously serious demeanour. "Do you have any questions?"

Silently, I shake my head, and pile all the papers together, sliding them to the middle of the table. She smiles, nods, and does the same with the file on her side. And after a few seconds, all of the papers and evidence go up in flames. I watch as the colours shift and change between red, orange, and blue. Then slowly dissipate to embers and finally ash.

"I would also just like to add," I raise my eyes, locking in on hers. "This is a kill-mission, though given your record I doubt you'll have much of a problem with it. But in the end I still need confirmation, do you understand your assignment?"

Without a word, I nod and she signals me to stand up and head out. I give her a slight bow, and with a deep breath, exit the office, making my way to the submarine across the way.

About The Author

Porscha Anne Aubrey is a teenage author that resides in Canada. Her dream is to be able to make a living from her writing as well as her podcast, Creative Writing Club. One of her other goals is to start her own charity where she gives out scholarships to students even if their grades aren't the best. That's mainly important to her because she believes that a student can have the drive to get a higher education but still be unable to get amazing grades due to their at-home life. Her other goal is to start her own publishing company and call it 'Creative Writing Club,' mainly just to go along with the brand of CWC that she's been using for so long, like when she started her own magazine.

For her entire life, Porscha has always enjoyed writing. From writing short stories, to poems, to scripts, and even starting some novel projects, she has worked hard on improving her craft. Though it wasn't till the start of ninth grade that she decided to take it more seriously and began writing 'Deathchill.' By 2021 the entire Deathchill trilogy has been completed, and she has moved on to other projects.

With the hopes that being an author is what she's meant to do, Porscha will continue to work hard and write towards her future.